Dear Reader,

Come with me to t
majestic Colorado
there is nothing to
and nothing but nature surrounding us.

Let me take you on a search-and-rescue mission
where we'll find danger and adventure, in a
place where civilization is merely a far-off
fantasy.

And let me introduce you to a strong-willed
woman who has been playing a starring role in
my disturbing dreams . . . and stirring feelings I
just don't trust. . . .

Cody Wolf

Colorado

DALLAS SCHULZE

Stormwalker

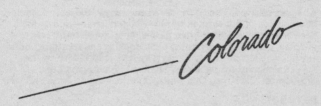

Harlequin Books

TORONTO • NEW YORK • LONDON
AMSTERDAM • PARIS • SYDNEY • HAMBURG
STOCKHOLM • ATHENS • TOKYO • MILAN
MADRID • WARSAW • BUDAPEST • AUCKLAND

HARLEQUIN ENTERPRISES LTD.
225 Duncan Mill Road, Don Mills,
Ontario, Canada M3B 3K9

STORMWALKER

ISBN: 0-373-45156-3

Published Harlequin Enterprises, Ltd. 1987, 1993

Prologue

The single-engine Cessna was coming in too low. The sleek red-and-white body barely skimmed over the mountain, almost brushing the treetops. There was an ominous catch in the engine—a missed beat in what should have been a smooth roar. Only an occasional mule deer heard the sound, cocking their graceful heads at this noisy invasion of their retreat before bounding deeper into the pine forests.

Heavy gray clouds formed a thick blanket over the mountains. The small plane bucked, fighting to retain some altitude. For a moment the nose tilted up, and it looked as if the plane might win the battle to stay airborne. But it was only a momentary victory.

The clouds seemed to press down on the fragile craft and it plummeted earthward. Struggling to keep its nose up, it twisted its way into a narrow valley. A wing sheared off against a granite wall. The craft spun away and continued its mad journey until the nose caught on a shallow ridge. The plane tilted upward, poised for a moment on its nose like an oddly graceful bird before tipping over, almost in slow motion, to land on the other side of the ridge.

The landing gear pointed uselessly into the air, the wheels spun madly until they gradually slowed and then came to a halt. Where moments before the mountains had been filled with the grinding of metal as the craft died, now there was only silence.

The mountains had seen many things. Death was not new. Death was the way in which all things returned to the earth that had borne them. Eventually, the metal of this strange creature would dissolve and flake into the soil. It might take decades or centuries, but the mountains had time.

The first snowfall of the season began to drift down, sifting a powdery covering over the gay red and white of the wreckage.

Chapter One

"You're not making any sense."

"I'm making perfect sense," Sara said firmly.

"What do you think you can do that the authorities haven't already done?"

"I'm going to find Cullen."

"See? You're not making any sense." David Turner paused in his pacing and faced her across the bed. "Stop packing for a minute and look at me."

Sara glanced up and smiled. "Don't try for the macho image, David. It doesn't suit you. I'm listening, but I have to finish packing or I'll miss the plane."

He glared at her for a moment before giving up. In the three years he had known Sara Grant, he had never yet managed to win an argument with her, except when it came to business. She was willing to listen to anything he had to say about her career, but on everything else she went her own way.

"Sara, be rational." He abandoned firm masculinity for an appeal to reason. "The search-and-rescue people in Colorado have already done everything possible."

"They've done everything they have the time to do," she said as she folded a pair of heavy jeans and laid them next to a stack of warm shirts.

He came around the end of the bed with the quick stride so characteristic of him and caught her hands, forcing her to abandon the suitcase and look at him.

"Honey, you're asking for more pain. It's been over a week since the plane went down. There's almost no chance anyone would still be alive."

"*Almost* no chance. It's the 'almost' that keeps me going, David." Her fingers tightened around his and she reined in her impatience to be gone, trying to make him understand how she felt. "I can't give up as long as there's any chance at all. If Cullen survived the crash, he's going to know that I'll find him. I can't let him down."

"You can't search the Rocky Mountains by yourself, honey. What are you going to do? The search-and-rescue people have already told you they can't do anything more."

"I don't know, but I'll think of something once I'm there."

"Let me come with you."

For the first time in days, her delicate features lit with a smile. "Now I know you really do love me. Only true love could possibly drag an offer like that out of you. You get hives at the very thought of the great outdoors. You're the only man I know who can zero in on poison oak and fall into the only patch of it in a hundred-mile radius. Thanks for the offer, but I wouldn't ask that of you. Besides, you've got commitments here."

She flexed her captive hands and he released them reluctantly. He watched her continue packing, feeling as if a chasm were opening up at his feet, separating them forever.

Sara sensed his despondence but there was nothing she could do about it. All her thoughts were centered on Cullen—on his need. It was almost as if he were calling to her, reaching across the miles between them. Her soft mouth set stubbornly. Cullen was alive, and she was going to find him come hell or high water.

She rolled a pair of thick socks and tucked them into a corner of the suitcase. Catching David's mournful expression, she gave him a strained smile. "It's not as if I'm going off without any plans at all. When I told John Larkin I was flying out to continue the search, he said that he could give me the name of someone who might agree to help me. He doesn't work cheap, but I don't care what it costs. I'll pay anything to find Cullen."

Her delicately plucked brows came together in a frown. "As soon as we get back, I'll apply for a second loan on the house. I just hope whoever he is, he'll be willing to wait on his money."

"Oh, hell, I'll give you the money." David ran his long, graceful fingers through his shaggy brown hair. "If I can't talk you out of going and you won't let me go with you, at least let me bankroll the expedition."

Sara stopped packing to look at him, blinking back the first tears since the crash. "Just a loan," she managed to say firmly.

"Just a loan. Look on me as your friendly neighborhood banker, eager to lend a helping hand." He gave her a crooked smile and reached out to cup his hand around her cheek. "I may think this whole thing is crazy, but I care about the boy too, you know. I hope you find him."

"Oh, David." His name was a choked whisper as she went into his arms, letting him hold her close. She rubbed her face against the soft cashmere of the sweater she'd given him for his birthday and inhaled the combination of scents she always associated with him: the pipe he'd started smoking when he gave up cigarettes, the cologne he always wore, a whiff of the chemicals he used to develop his pictures. This last thought made her smile. No matter what the occasion, or how elegant his clothing, David always smelled like a photographer. Sometimes she had the whimsical idea that if they ever X-rayed him, they were going to find a jumble of camera parts.

She pulled away, dabbing at her eyes. "You shouldn't be so nice. You'll make me cry and you know how you hate red eyes."

His thumb tilted her chin up, and he looked down into her face, his expression brooding. "You would be the most beautiful woman in the world, even with red eyes."

Sara smiled up at him, uncertain in the face of his intensity. David Turner usually reserved that emotion for his work. Away from the cameras and his studio, he was the perfect laid-back Californian.

"It's nice to know you feel that way, but I doubt if your clients would agree. It's hard to sell mascara when the model's eyes look like she's been on an all-night binge."

Whatever strange mood had gripped him, he seemed to shake it off. His hand dropped away from her face. "You can always fall back on selling nail polish, unless your hands get red when you cry, too."

"Not that I've noticed." She turned back to the suitcase, pushing aside his odd mood as she quickly tucked in the last few items and shut the lid, snapping the latches closed. "I think I've packed everything I'm likely to need. I'll buy anything I've forgotten once I know what I'm up against."

She let David carry the suitcase out to her car, sensing his need to help in this small way. But she was firm in her refusal to let him drive her to the airport. "I can park the car in long-term parking. You've got a shoot scheduled this afternoon. You don't have time to run me to the airport."

"I can cancel it."

"There's no reason to."

"I just feel like I should do something useful."

"David, you're doing something immensely useful in offering me a loan if I need it. I have no idea who this guy is that John Larkin thinks might help me. I may need to lay my hands on the cash right away."

Reluctantly, he lifted the suitcase into the trunk of her compact car. Impatient to be gone but sensing his need for reassurance, Sara sought for the right words. "I really do appreciate the loan, David. It's going to make things a lot easier for me."

"No problem. I'll instruct my bank to let you draw whatever you need." His hands came up to catch her by the shoulders, his fingers pressing into the soft fabric of her shirt. "Take care of yourself."

"I will. Don't look so worried. I'm not going to do anything stupid."

"See that you don't."

She raised her head as he drew her closer. There was a strange desperation in his kiss, as if he expected it to be their last. She responded by putting her arms around his neck and holding him close, offering him reassurance without words. When he drew back, his eyes searched her face intently for a moment, asking questions she couldn't read.

"I'd better get going." She didn't understand his mood, but at the moment she didn't have the emotional strength to question it. All her emotions were tied up with Cullen. There was little left to offer David.

She slid into the driver's seat and started the car. "I'll call you as soon as I know anything. It may take some time, so don't worry if you don't hear from me right away."

He leaned in the window and planted a hard kiss on her mouth before stepping away from the car. "Take care."

She backed out of the driveway, lifting her hand in a brief farewell. David stood on the small lawn and watched until the little red car turned a corner and was out of sight. He hunched his shoulders against the cool autumn breeze, his slender hands shoved deep into the pockets of his jeans as he stared after her.

Why did he have the feeling that they'd just said goodbye forever?

HE CAME AWAKE SUDDENLY, instantly alert and on guard, as if there were danger nearby. For a moment he lay absolutely still, absorbing the silence of the old house. He relaxed slightly. There was nothing nearby.

He swept back the light blanket, which was his only concession to the autumn chill, and swung his feet to the floor. He stood up, arching his back in a light stretch. He was not going back to sleep, and lying in bed wouldn't change that. It was time he was up anyway. He left the bedroom and moved through the dim house easily, his bare feet making no sound on the worn hardwood floors. In the kitchen he stirred the coals in the old wood-burning stove, which provided both food and heat in the winter.

Sullen light caught on his sharply chiseled features. A wide forehead, dark brows, a nose that stopped just short of hawkish and a sensually molded mouth above a strong jaw covered with dark stubble. Heavy black hair cut with shaggy disregard for style and worn just a little too long fell onto his forehead. Thick black lashes shielded eyes of a startlingly dark and brilliant emerald green.

Crouched in front of the fire, he was a figure more pagan than modern. The light flickered over a lean body, a muscled chest lightly dusted with curling hair, corded thighs that lifted him easily upright as he slammed the firebox shut and stretched again. Morning's first tentative light slid over the rise to the east and slipped in through the uncurtained window, gilding his naked frame, adding a golden glow to the warm coppery tint of his skin.

He turned to the window and lifted his hand as if to capture the fleeting rays of dawn that sifted through his fingers. With a half smile, he turned away and began to prepare the morning coffee, carefully grinding the beans and setting them to brew with a care that would have seemed appropriate at a gourmet restaurant. In the scuffed-wood surroundings of the worn kitchen, the modern whir of the grinder was as out of place as a rocket launcher next to a covered wagon.

With the aroma of coffee filling the room, he crossed the buckled linoleum floor to the back door. The hinges squealed a protest as he opened the door and went out onto the porch. His hands leaned on the rail, his eyes never leaving the mountains that loomed across the valley.

Something was wrong up there. The dream that had awakened him so abruptly had left him with only fleeting images of twisted metal and towering peaks. A plane crash. The faint shudder that twitched his shoulders had nothing to do with the chill in the air. Whatever had happened, it was going to have an impact on his life. His nostrils flared slightly as if he could smell change on the wind.

With a faint shrug, he turned away from the silent mountains. Whatever was going to happen had already been set in motion. There was nothing he could do to change it. He pushed the door shut behind him, shutting out the mountains and the dream images of tortured wreckage and eyes the color of mountain columbines.

SARA FORCED HER HANDS to ease their death grip and relax on the arms of her seat. The DC-10 taxied smoothly down the runway toward the terminal and she began to feel as if she could breathe again. She had never liked flying. Even as a child she had felt vulnerable suspended in midair with only a thin metal shell between her and the clouds.

When her brother, Evan, and his wife died in a plane crash when Sara was twenty-three years old, it had confirmed her distrust of the machines. She had never been able to understand how Evan's son could retain his love of flying, but she hadn't tried to discourage him. Now another plane was down, and she might have lost her nephew. He was all she had left and he might be dead.

She shook her head as the people around her began to gather up briefcases and overnight bags. She had to think positively. Cullen was alive. All she had to do was find him.

She exited the plane with a feeling of having beat the odds. Only the urgent need for speed had driven her to get on the gleaming monster, and she felt a certain sense of triumph at having arrived safely. Cullen would laugh when she told him how she'd felt.

She followed the crowd toward the luggage pickup area. Her boot heels clicked briskly on the hard floors as she wove her way around strollers and luggage carts. She waited impatiently for her dark brown suitcase to appear on the carousel. When it finally arrived, she stepped forward to lift it off, only to find herself forestalled by a middle-aged man wearing a suit complete with cowboy boots and Western string tie.

She summoned up a smile and a murmur of thanks, shaking her head politely when he offered to carry her luggage to her car. She lifted the heavy suitcase easily and headed for the car rental booths. She was used to men who thought she needed protection. At five-foot-two, Sara had a slim, fragile look that made men think of delicate flowers. She capitalized on that look for her modeling, but she was more than capable of carrying her own luggage.

It seemed to take forever to rent a four-wheel-drive vehicle and get out of the airport. It was early evening before she pulled the truck to a halt in front of the small tract home in a suburb of Denver. She had called from the airport and John Larkin had given her directions to his home.

Walking up the path to the front door, Sara zipped up her jacket. It was a lot colder in Denver than it had been in Los Angeles. She tried not to think abo t how much colder it would be in the mountains that loomed above the city. Cullen had been camping all his life. He would know how to keep warm.

John Larkin was a rather ordinary looking man in his late thirties. Somehow, Sara had been expecting someone who looked more like Indiana Jones, complete with battered hat. His leadership of a search-and-rescue team had conjured up visions of derring-do and adventure that didn't quite suit the smallish, slightly balding man who introduced her to his wife and baby son.

"We have a rough idea of where the plane went down, but we couldn't see any sign of it from the air. It must have gone down somewhere in this general vicinity, judging from the last radio contact they made."

He drew a red circle around a dauntingly large portion of the map that lay spread out on the dining room table. Sara took a sip of her coffee, trying not to be discouraged by the size of the area he had marked.

"Why couldn't you find the wreckage?"

He shrugged. "That's a big area. There are a lot of canyons and valleys. We covered the area by air, but there's always the possibility that we missed the crash site. More likely, the plane's out of sight under an overhang, or resting so close against a cliff that the shadows would keep it hidden. And the high country is getting the first snows of the season. Nothing too deep yet, but even a light snow layer would cover the wreck enough to blend it in with the scenery."

He sat back and picked up his coffee cup, letting her digest what he had told her for a moment before he spoke again. "I have to be honest with you, Ms Grant. I don't think there's much chance of any survivors.

Small plane crashes..." His voice trailed off and he shrugged. "I'm afraid even if your son survived the crash, there's not much chance of him surviving for very long alone in the mountains. A kid his age..." Again he let the sentence finish itself.

"He's not my son. Cullen is my nephew, and he's a wilderness freak. He and Bill, the man who was flying the plane, have been going on hunting and camping trips since Cullen was ten years old. That's eight years of experience. I think he's still alive."

John Larkin shrugged. "I can't blame you for hoping. I wish we could do more, but we've had several lost hikers and another light-plane crash to contend with. Our people will continue to keep an eye out for any sign of the plane, but we just don't have the men to keep looking full-time."

"I understand." Sara finished her coffee. "On the phone you said that you could give me the name of someone who might be able to help me."

He nodded reluctantly. "Actually, it was my wife who thought of him. He's found a couple of crash sites that we'd given up on. No survivors in either one, but he did find the sites. He's not very sociable. He's refused to work with us on any official basis, but he knows the area where your nephew's plane went down and he might be willing to help you."

"I'll try anything. What's his name and how do I find him?"

"Wolf. That's the only name I've ever heard. Don't know whether it's first or last. He raises horses just this side of the Wyoming border. In fact, his place isn't far from where we think the plane went down. He doesn't have a phone, but I can tell you how to get there."

Sara glanced at her watch. "I suppose it's too late to start tonight," she said reluctantly.

"Best to start first thing in the morning," he said.

Janet Larkin entered the room on her husband's words. "You can sleep here tonight," she said. "The sofa opens out into a bed."

"I don't want to put you to any trouble."

Janet waved away Sara's protest. "It's no problem. There's no sense in you trying to scare up a place to sleep when we've got room here."

Exhaustion swept over Sara in a wave so powerful that it was suddenly almost impossible to summon up the energy to speak. "Thank you. I really appreciate this."

"Tomorrow morning, you'll be fresh and ready to tackle the drive."

"More likely, she'll need to be fresh to tackle Wolf," John muttered.

Chapter Two

The route Sara took the next morning skirted along the foothills of the Rocky Mountains. When she turned off the interstate onto the less-traveled highway, the mountains sat squarely in front of her, dominating her field of vision as she drew closer.

They were beautiful, aloof, unconquered, magnificent... and deadly. She thrust the insidious thought away. She would not let herself think in those terms. She had to keep believing that Cullen was alive.

It was early afternoon when she turned off the main road onto a narrow dirt lane, which she hoped would lead her to the mysterious Wolf. The road dipped down, enclosing her between bluffs of red sandstone. She shifted gears as the road began a shallow climb and suddenly she was at the top of the incline.

Despite the circumstances, she could not help but release a gasp of appreciation. Right in front of her was an old-fashioned wooden gate that arched high overhead. At the top of the gate hung a sign with a brand burned into it announcing pictorially that this was the Arrow Bar W Ranch. A sign hung on the barbed wire fence to the right of the gate announcing that no hunting was allowed.

Through the gate, Sara could see the land spread out in a verdant carpet of fall grasses. A mile or so from where she was, a rambling house sprawled lazily in the crisp sunshine. A barn and several outbuildings stood off to the right. Beyond the house the green valley floor widened between more of the red sandstone bluffs. From this distance, it looked as smooth and lustrous as a carpet that rolled across the gradually rising land until it disappeared beneath the darker green of the pine forest that covered the lower slopes of the mountains.

And the mountains themselves. If she had thought them omnipresent before, she realized now that what she had seen before had been only a sample of what they could be. Here they dominated the landscape, overshadowing the jewellike valley while at the same time seeming to shelter it. Like a mother protecting a child.

She shook her head and took her foot off the brake. She hadn't even been aware of stopping until that moment. She drove over the cattle guard beneath the gate and started down into the valley. For some reason, the sight of the peaceful valley nestled so snugly among the mountains made them seem less threatening and renewed her hope for Cullen.

She pulled the truck to a halt in front of the house and climbed out hesitantly. Gravel crunched beneath her boots as she approached the wide porch that wrapped around the front of the building. Flower beds flanked either side of the steps, the last of the summer's marigolds glowing orange and yellow against the gray of the weathered wood facade.

The front door was open and she knocked on the screen door, trying to resist the urge to peek through the patched screening and into the house. There probably wasn't much need for locked doors this far from civilization and the crime that went with it.

She glanced around while she waited for some response to her knock. An old-fashioned porch swing was suspended across one end of the porch. It looked much newer than the house, and she wondered if there was a Mrs. Wolf. The swing and the flowers seemed to be decidedly feminine touches, and Sara began to revise her image of a crusty old mountain man.

She knocked again, and this time she peered through the door, tentatively calling out a soft hello. There had been a truck parked next to the barn, which seemed to indicate that someone was home, but he obviously was not in the house. With a sigh, she knocked one last time. She hoped that she could find someone without searching the entire ranch. Maybe he was in the barn feeding horses or stacking hay or something. She turned away from the door, her eyes skimming over the swing again as she moved toward the porch steps.

She came to an abrupt halt, automatically steadying herself with one hand against the railing. The man who stood at the bottom of the steps could have come from a painting of a different time. A dusty brown cowboy hat was tilted slightly back over casually cut black hair that brushed the back of his collar. His shirt was of plain blue cotton and, like his jeans, it looked as if it had been softened by years of washing.

But, instead of the boots that should have completed the look, the bottoms of his jeans disappeared into suede moccasins that looked as if they had been molded to his feet. Leather thongs laced the soft boots to his legs. The moccasins and his almost hawk-like facial features made him look as if he were composed of two pictures, one over the other—the cowboy barely covering the savage underneath.

Was this the Wolf she had come to find, or was he a drifter with no business being here?

"May I help you?" The polite question added the final contrast to his image.

Sara cleared her throat. "Are you Wolf?" She brought the name out hesitantly, realizing that it fit him all too well. There was something lean and tough about him.

"I'm Wolf." The flat statement hung on the still air between them. He didn't add to it. Didn't ask her why she was looking for him. He just watched her with eyes shadowed by the brim of his hat.

Sara drew in a deep breath and moved down the steps until she stood on the second one from the bottom, her face level with his. He didn't move away as she drew nearer, but she sensed a barrier going up between them, like a clear wall that said "only so far and no closer."

"I'm Sara Grant."

She held out her hand. His eyes lowered from her face to the delicate contours of her hand and, for a moment, she thought he was going to ignore her gesture. Slowly, his hand came up and he clasped her fingers. For the brief instant that his palm held hers, Sara had the sensation of having touched something intensely alive.

She drew her hand away, slightly shaken by the sensation, and rubbed her fingers unconsciously across her palm, as if she could still feel the callused strength of his hand. Wolf's eyes narrowed on the gesture.

Uncertain in the face of his continued silence, Sara spoke again. "John Larkin gave me your name. He seemed to think you might be able to help me."

"I'm sure John was wildly enthusiastic about your contacting me." The words were spoken with an undertone of irony that confused her.

"Actually, it was his wife who thought of you."

"I'm sure it was." He studied her silently for a moment, and Sara had the urge to reach out and tug the hat off his head so that she could really see his eyes.

As if he'd read her thought, he pulled off his hat and stepped around her. "Come in and you can tell me why you thought I might be able to help you."

She followed him up the stairs and into the house. His hat sailed onto a table in the living room. Sara quickened her pace to keep up with him, trying to take in her surroundings as she went. She got only a glimpse of the living room—heavy furniture and a huge painting on one wall—before he led the way through a wide door and into the kitchen.

"Coffee?"

"That would be nice, thank you."

She sat down at the table, resting her hands on the battered Formica top. His movements were easy, almost fluid, as he reached for cups and poured the fragrant liquid from a coffee maker that looked like the last word in high tech. A few feet away, a cast-iron pot simmered on top of the wood-burning stove, releasing the appetizing scent of stew.

Contrasts. He seemed to be a man of contrasts. A cowboy hat and Indian moccasins, weathered boards and flower beds, high-tech coffee and a wood-burning stove. What next?

He set the cups on the table and then sat down opposite her. "I can offer you sugar, but I'm afraid all I have is canned milk."

"That's okay. I prefer it black." She took a sip. "It's very good."

"Jamaican. I order the beans from back East."

She lifted her gaze to his face and then forgot what she had intended to say. Contrast. The warm copper of his skin against eyes so green they dazzled. Heavy, straight black lashes surrounded them, emphasizing their extraordinary color.

She flushed wildly and lowered her eyes when he arched a dark brow in slow inquiry. A swallow of coffee gave her a few seconds to regain her composure.

"Mr...er...Wolf."

"Cody. You seem uneasy with my last name."

"Well, actually, it's not that. I just wasn't sure if it was your last name or your first."

"Why did Larkin send you here?"

Sara almost sighed with relief. There was something about this man that confused her. She seemed to be having a hard time keeping control of the conversation.

"He said that you've been able to locate two crash sites that search and rescue couldn't find. I—"

"No."

Sara stopped in midsentence and stared at him.

"No? You haven't even heard what I'm going to ask."

"You want me to find the plane that crashed near here ten days ago. No."

"Near here? Did you see it? Do you know where it is?"

Cody hardened himself against the hope in her voice, the eagerness in her eyes. Eyes he had seen before. In a dream.

"I didn't see it and I don't know where it is. I listen to the radio, and there have been a lot of search planes going through. It was pretty easy to conclude that it must have crashed in this area." He didn't mention the dream that told him about the crash long before the radio had. That was something he didn't share with anyone. Certainly not with this fragile-looking woman with hair the color of golden silk and columbine eyes.

"John seemed to think you might help. He said—"

"He was wrong. I'm sorry you made the trip for nothing." He was on his feet and on his way out the door before Sara had a chance to say anything. The door had shut behind him by the time she got to her feet. When she got to the door, there was no sign of him. But that didn't stop her.

Along with her concern for Cullen, a healthy anger began to sizzle. Cody Wolf wasn't to get rid of her so easily. He'd help her whether he wanted to or not.

CODY FELT HER COMING long before he heard the rapid scrunch of gravel crushed beneath her narrow boots. He pulled the brush a little more rapidly across Dancer's coat, causing the stallion to live up to his name as he danced uneasily away from the shimmering tension that surrounded his owner.

Cody murmured to the horse softly in a mixture of languages, forcing his hand into a steady stroking motion until the bay stilled beneath his touch. The barn door creaked open, the wail of hinges an appropriate accompaniment to the slim storm that blew in wearing the guise of a woman.

"Our conversation is not finished, Mr. Wolf. After making this miserable trip out here, I think courtesy demands that you at least hear me out."

"Do you?" His hand didn't pause. He didn't want to hear her out. She was a danger to everything he'd worked for. He didn't know how or why, but she threatened his plans.

Sara stared at him for a moment without speaking, reading in that impassive expression the collapse of her last hope of finding Cullen. If he refused her, she was left with nowhere to turn. Cullen was in those mountains somewhere, maybe hurt and needing her, and she couldn't get to him.

The extended silence finally drove Cody to look at her, and he muttered a curse. Her eyes shimmered with tears. He wanted to dismiss it as a trick. A woman's weapon to gain sympathy. But her teeth bit deep into her lower lip and there was a look of pride in her expression that told him she hated this display of weakness.

"Hell." He wrapped his hand in Dancer's mane and backed the stallion out of the stall. A pat on the rump sent the big horse out the side door and into the corral on the side of the barn.

"Tell me why you came to me."

In the dim light of the barn, it was impossible to read his expression. He must have picked up his hat on the way out of the house because it was once again shielding his eyes. Sara thought she could read reluctant sympathy in his voice, and for a moment her pride rebelled. She despised women who used tears to get their way. But pride was irrelevant beside her need. Without him, she didn't have a chance of finding Cullen.

She glanced around for a seat. There was nothing available to sit on except bales of hay, and she sat on one without complaint. The last week and a half had been draining, and even the scratchy support of the hay felt wonderful.

"Ten days ago, a single-engine Cessna went down in the mountains somewhere in this general vicinity. The search-and-rescue people have done everything they can, but they haven't been able to find the crash site. John Larkin said that you've had some luck finding a couple of planes they'd given up on."

"Did he also tell you that there were no survivors in either of those crashes?" There was an emotion in his voice that she couldn't define. Her eyes narrowed, but he was little more than a silhouette against the open door behind him. One shoulder rested against the edge of a stall. His pose was suggestive of ease, even indolence, but she was sure that wasn't what he was feeling.

"He told me," she admitted.

"But you still want me to find the crash."

"Cullen isn't dead." It was a flat statement.

Cody took in the stubborn angle of her jaw and swallowed the urge to curse long and loud. "Small-plane crashes do not result in a lot of survivors." He tried to keep his voice reasonable but firm. "It's been ten days since it happened. Even if anyone survived the crash, ten days in the high country is enough to kill even an uninjured man."

"I know that, but I also know that Cullen is alive."

Cullen. Her husband? The thought brought a confusing mixture of feelings. Something in him rejected the thought of her belonging to another man, and yet, if she were married, what possible threat could she offer to him?

"Ms Grant, I wish I could help you, but I think you're just going to have to accept the fact that your husband is..."

"Cullen is my nephew and I'm not going to accept anything except that he's alive and waiting to be rescued."

Cody tugged his hat off and slapped it idly against his thigh, uncertain whether he was glad or sorry that it wasn't a husband she was trying to find.

"Your nephew? That makes it even more unlikely that he'd survive. If we assume he made it through the crash uninjured, which isn't likely, he'd have been alone with a dead or badly injured pilot. The mountains can be very unsympathetic, Ms Grant."

"Cullen isn't a little boy. He's eighteen and his hobby is wilderness survival. He's been camping and hunting since he was a child."

"Even so..."

"Cullen is a survivor. And the man who was flying the plane also knows what he's doing. If any two people have a chance, Bill and Cullen do. I can't just give up on them."

"There's such a thing as facing reality. The high country has already had the first snows of the season. Even two experts in survival would be hard-pressed to keep warm, especially if one or both of them were injured, which is almost inevitable."

He shook his head and stood away from the post. "I'm sorry, Ms Grant, but I've got a ranch to run. I can't help you."

"Ten thousand dollars."

Cody froze, half turned away from her. Outside, a meadowlark called musically. Through the open door, he could see Dancer rubbing his shoulder against a convenient fence post. The barn was silent. He had the feeling that she was holding her breath. Slowly, he turned to look at her.

"What?"

"You heard me. Ten thousand dollars to look for my nephew."

It shouldn't be possible for such a delicately feminine jaw to look so hard. Everything about her, from the fragile angles of her face to the slender curves of her body, spoke of helpless femininity. Everything except the angle of her jaw and the determination in those amethyst eyes.

"I don't think..."

"Fifteen thousand. Fifteen to look for him and twenty-five if you find the wreckage. Whether he's dead or alive."

"You don't..."

Sara got to her feet and moved closer. Cody inhaled the warm floral fragrance of her perfume and wondered if it was possible to be drugged by a scent. She tilted her head until she could look straight into his eyes. Even with her boots on, her head just reached his chin, but she seemed unaware of her disadvantage.

"I don't know much about ranching, but I do know that everything costs a lot of money these days." She spoke rapidly, her desperate need to persuade him giving her speech a staccato ring. "Think of all the things twenty-five thousand dollars would buy. It could make a big difference in a small operation."

Cody raised one eyebrow, trying to decide if he was angry that she was trying to buy him, or if he admired her stubborn persistence.

"But it could be only fifteen thousand," he murmured softly, suppressing a twinge of shame for baiting her.

"It will be twenty-five." She spoke with absolute confidence.

"That's a lot of money."

"Don't worry. I have it, and if you want more, I'll get that."

"I'm sure that won't be necessary."

"Then you'll do it?" There was so much hope, so much need in the question that Cody found himself temporizing instead of just giving her a flat no.

"Let me think about it."

"Think about it!" Sara caught herself before she said anything else. When she spoke again, her words were carefully chosen. "It's already been ten days, Mr. Wolf. There really isn't a whole lot of time in which to think about it."

"I have a fence to check. Why don't you go into the house and have some coffee and read a magazine or something and I'll be back in a couple of hours?" He was lifting a saddle off a rack as he spoke.

Sara bit back the urge to scream at him that she had to have an answer now. They'd come from absolute refusal to at least a possibility that he'd help her. Realistically, two hours wasn't going to make any difference. She drew on the hours she had spent smiling for the camera no matter how she felt and forced her lips to curve.

"All right."

Cody thought he'd seen grizzly bears with more-sincere smiles, but he gave her points for self-control. He watched her turn and walk away, his eyes skimming over the slim lines of her back, and his admiration was tinged with a purely masculine appreciation of the female shape of her. In snug jeans, tucked into black boots, her derriere was delightfully inviting. And the bulky warmth of a periwinkle-colored sweater didn't disguise the graceful curve of waist and bust.

Small but nicely formed, he admitted reluctantly. He carried the saddle out into the corral and draped it over a section of fence. A sharp whistle brought Dancer over to him, and he ran his hand along the proud arch of the stallion's neck.

"And worlds apart from us, boy," he whispered softly. Dancer nodded his head in apparent agreement and pushed his nose demandingly against Cody's shoulder. A smile broke the frown between the man's brows and he laughed softly. "You're right. I shouldn't have called you over here just to chat."

A few minutes later, he leaned down to open the corral gate and then shut it with his foot once they were through. He turned the stallion up the valley and urged him into a gentle canter. The saddle still lay on the fence. The only thing between man and horse was the softness of a saddle blanket.

Cody could feel the horse's powerful muscles rippling between his knees as the bay paced across the grass. Checking fences could be done another day. Right now, he needed to think.

He let Dancer find his own path, his eyes skimming over the land as the horse slowed to a walk. She'd certainly hit the nail on the head when she said that ranching cost a lot. He wasn't broke, but it was going to take time to build up a reputation for his horses. In a few years he'd be able to sell every foal he produced, but in the meantime ...

Twenty-five thousand dollars would go a long way, but that wasn't the reason that he was thinking about her proposition. She was so sure the boy was alive. What if she was right? Could he take that chance? And then there was the dream. Twice before he had dreamed, and each time he'd gone into the mountains to find death. He didn't want that again. But what if the boy was alive?

SARA RESTLESSLY PACED back and forth on the porch. What was she going to do if he came back and still refused to help her? No, she wasn't even going to think of that. Cody Wolf was the best chance she had of finding Cullen and he was going to help her. She had to believe that.

The air was taking on a distinctly chilly edge, and she shoved her hands into the pockets of her jeans. She stopped pacing to lean against the porch rail, casting a glance over her shoulder at the screen door. It would be warm in the house.

When she first left Cody at the barn, she had accepted his invitation to wait in the house. But she hadn't stayed there long. The painting she had only glimpsed earlier hung in a prominent position on one wall. At least four feet by six feet, its very size would have made it a focal point. But it was the subject matter of the painting that caused it to dominate the room.

Against a snowy background, a lone wolf stood braced, its head turned to look out of the canvas. The artist had captured every magnificent aspect of the creature, from the heavy winter coat that was just a few shades darker than the snow that surrounded it to the look of wary intelligence in the golden eyes.

It was the eyes that had finally driven Sara onto the porch. At first, she had sat down across from the painting, admiring the artist's skill. Then she had picked up an issue of *National Geographic* and started to flip through it, not really reading but glancing at the pictures and skimming an article or two. After a few minutes, she began to feel as if she were being watched.

She tried to dismiss the sensation but it just kept growing. Feeling like an idiot, she had moved to a chair off to the side. It was a tribute to the artist that the wolf actually seemed to be looking at her. But the sensation didn't go away, and she looked up impatiently to find that the wolf's eyes still seemed to be focused right on her.

She quickly discovered that those eyes followed her no matter where she was in the room, watching her as if real intelligence lay beneath the painted canvas. Feeling like a total fool, she abandoned the living room and retreated onto the porch. She could admire the artist's skill, but right now her nerves were in no condition to deal with those watching eyes.

It seemed as if eons had passed, but it couldn't have been more than an hour or two before Cody returned. She had abandoned pacing in favor of the porch swing. One foot pushed against the worn planking of the floor, setting the swing into creaky motion. With her eyes closed, she concentrated on making each breath slow and deep, trying to block out every thought. It was a simple relaxation technique that had made it easier for her to tolerate the inevitable delays a model faced: waiting for props to be set up, waiting for garments that had mysteriously disappeared to be found.

As Cody came up the steps and onto the porch, she reminded him more than ever of a delicate mountain flower. The periwinkle of her sweater and the honey-gold of her hair, which fell in easy curls onto her shoulders, were bright spots of color against the weathered house.

She stirred up emotions that he didn't trust. Not just desire—that was inevitable and could be dealt with. But he found himself wanting to just hold her and reassure her. He wanted to sit down next to her and stroke her hair and tell her not to worry about anything. Those feelings were not so easily categorized and filed away. And that disturbed him.

Sara opened her eyes slowly, feeling more relaxed than she had since the crash. The sun had slipped behind the mountains, leaving the valley dusky with evening light. Cody was little more than a silhouette in front of her, a shoulder casually braced against one of the posts that supported the porch roof, his hat tilted back on his head. She couldn't see his eyes but she knew he was looking at her.

With his silent arrival, tension was suddenly a living presence. She sat up, swallowing the urge to demand his decision instantly. She couldn't allow herself to have any doubts about it. He had to agree to help her find Cullen. Anything else was unthinkable.

Cody tugged his hat off, slapping it against his thigh as he looked at her. A moment ago she had looked as if she hadn't a care in the world. Now every line of her body bespoke tension. Cursing himself for nine kinds of a fool, he made the only choice he could.

"I'll find your nephew."

Not "I'll try" but "I'll find," Sara noted with the part of her mind that was still capable of functioning. Everything else was blanked out by a tremendous relief.

He was going to help her find Cullen. It was going to be all right.

The Survivor

CULLEN SETTLED the last rock into place and stood up. At his feet was a shallow mound of dirt and rock. Not much to show for forty-five years of life. Bill Taylor had been a friend of Cullen's father before Cullen was

born. After Evan's death, Bill had in some ways filled
the gap he'd left behind. Bill had been a friend, camping buddy and teacher.

Cullen ground his teeth and then wiped one gloved
hand roughly across his cheek. He wasn't ashamed of
the tears. Bill had been a good friend. Tears were a
small tribute to that friendship. But right now survival
had to be his first priority. Bill would have been the
first to tell him that.

He stared at the grave a moment longer and then
lifted his hand in a half salute that acknowledged his
friend's military background.

"I'm sorry, Bill. I did what I could," he whispered
huskily. But first aid couldn't do much for a crushed
chest and fractured skull. The older man had never regained consciousness. Less than twenty-four hours after the plane went down, he had died quietly.

Cullen cocked his head, listening to the far-off whir
of a plane. Too far off, he decided immediately. Too
far off and fading already. He turned his collar up over
his ears. It had taken most of the day to scoop out the
shallow grave and cover it over with dirt and rocks. The
sun was dropping behind the mountain peaks and the
temperature would drop along with it. Twenty yards
behind him was the twisted wreckage of the plane. It
would offer some shelter.

Taking one last look at the grave, he turned away
and started toward the plane. His limping stride made
scuffed patterns in the light snowfall. *Just enough snow
to make life difficult*, he thought.

By the time he sank down in the shelter of the
wreckage, a faint sheen of sweat coated his features.
Only a miracle had prevented him from sharing Bill's
fate, but he hadn't come away from the crash scot-free.
A long, narrow cut skated its way down his face, more

annoying than life-threatening, but making any facial movement painful. Every muscle in his body felt as if it had been jarred loose by the impact, but he had been incredibly lucky.

The only major damage was to his left knee, and he had no way of knowing just how major that damage was. The joint was badly swollen and bending it was almost a thing of the past. He worked the leg of his pants up past the joint, drawing in a sharp breath as he shifted his leg in an attempt to get a better look at his knee.

His expression didn't change as he examined the swollen purple mass that bore little resemblance to a knee. He eased the fabric back down and leaned back against the fuselage. It had been almost forty-eight hours since the crash, and in that time he'd had little sleep. In a minute, he would get up and pull himself into his sleeping bag. He could pile Bill's on top and that would keep him warm enough tonight. Tomorrow he could try to decide what the next step was, but for now sleep was all he was capable of.

In a minute, he'd move. Right now, all he could do was be thankful that he was still alive.

Chapter Three

Cody dished stew onto two plates and set them on the table. His eyes flickered to the kitchen door. He had spent so much time alone that having someone else in the house felt like an invasion. He opened the oven to check on the loaf of bread that was warming and slammed the door with more force than necessary.

She was trouble. Every nerve in his body told him that. Just as every nerve in his body responded when she came near. He didn't need this. Not now. Not ever. He wanted to send her packing before she could demolish his carefully arranged life. But he couldn't. If the boy was alive, he had to find him.

And something told him that he couldn't just walk away from Sara Grant. He had to meet her challenge head-on. Meet it and conquer it.

He had his back to the door when she entered, but he knew that she was there. It was nothing so definite as a scent. It was almost as if her presence changed the very air he was breathing.

"It smells wonderful."

"Just stew," he said laconically. "Water okay?"

"Fine."

Sara sat down and waited until he was seated opposite her before picking up her fork. Ever since the crash her appetite had been nonexistent, but the rich scent of the stew made her stomach rumble.

She blushed, hoping he hadn't heard the embarrassingly eager sound. The food tasted even better than it smelled: dark chunks of beef swimming in a rich gravy with thick chunks of vegetables, and warm bread to catch every last drop. She chewed the first bite slowly, thinking that food had never tasted so good.

"It's wonderful," she told him sincerely.

He lifted a brow. "Just stew."

That seemed to be the extent of his interest in conversation for a while, and Sara was content to concentrate on her food.

"Where are you from?" he asked. She swallowed quickly, startled by the sudden question.

"L.A."

"What about the boy's parents? Why aren't they here harassing me into looking for him?"

"I didn't harass you. We have a business arrangement."

"I stand corrected." There was more than a tinge of irony in his words. "His parents?"

"My brother and his wife died in a light-plane crash five years ago."

"You must have been very young. Did you take the boy in?"

"I was twenty-three. There was no one else, even if I hadn't wanted him, which I did."

"A lot of responsibility." He wondered why he was probing like this. Did he really want to know anything more about her and the boy? The more he knew, the more real they became. And the harder it would be to hold them at a distance.

"My parents died when I was eight. Mom had a stroke, and a few months later Dad got pneumonia and died. I guess he just didn't have the willpower to fight. My brother, Evan, had just gotten married, but he and Alicia took me in without hesitation." Sara drew idle patterns on the scratched surface of the table, her eyes focused on the movement, her thoughts turned inward.

"Cullen has been more of a little brother than a nephew. And in the last couple of years, he's grown to be my best friend. He's one of those kids who seem to be born old. He's always known what he wanted to do and why. He's truly special."

She broke off, her voice cracking slightly on the last word. Talking about Cullen made the situation all the more frightening.

Cody swallowed the last bite of stew, and with it the urge to offer her reassurance. In his mind's eye, he could see those other crashes. The people he'd been too late to help. All he was likely to be bringing back to her was a body, and he wouldn't promise otherwise.

"What do you do in L.A.?" He asked the question to distract her from her thoughts and then he frowned inwardly. Why should he care about what her thoughts were? Damn it, he didn't want to know more about her. Did he?

Sara dragged her mind back to the present. "I'm a model."

"I thought models had to be very tall and thin." His thoughts were not really on what he was saying. She had taken off the bulky sweater and replaced it with a midnight-blue shirt. All through the meal, he had been trying not to look at her, resisting the pull of her. Now, she looked up with a half smile and their eyes met briefly. He could not drag his gaze away. In the back of his mind he wondered what his ancestors would have called someone who's eyes changed colors like the leaves in autumn. Witch?

Almost purple this afternoon, tonight her eyes were a deep blue, reflecting the color of her shirt. His thoughts faded for a moment and he was hardly aware of the silence that grew between them, matching the silence in the valley outside.

Sara felt as if her mind had stopped functioning, as if there was not a single thought in it that didn't spin around the man opposite her. Contrasts. His brusque refusal to help her, then his sudden acceptance. And she didn't think it had anything to do with the money. Something else had made him change his mind. He had practically ignored her existence all evening, yet now the look in his eyes spoke of total awareness.

He dragged his gaze away, and Sara was released from the spell that had wound them together. She cleared her throat and lowered her eyes to her plate, trying to remember what had been said just before that moment of silent communication. Oh, yes.

"Most models are a lot taller than I am." Her voice shook at first and then gradually steadied. "I do some modeling for catalogs and boutiques that specialize in petite sizes, but most of my work is hands and eyes. I've modeled various brands of eye shadow and nail polish. Some lotions. A lot of jewelry where all you see is my hands."

Cody listened to her with half an ear. His eyes were focused on the slender grace of her hands. Delicate bones and long, narrow fingers, the nails—not long, but not short—painted a pale pink. He wondered what it would be like to feel those hands on his body, those nails digging into his shoulders as she arched beneath him. And what color would those incredible eyes be when she was caught up in passion?

As if summoned from memory, he could see them. A hot, smoky gray. Lids half closed, her soft mouth damp from his kisses, her golden hair flowing like satin across a pillow. Not just any pillow, but his pillow. Her mouth swollen from his kisses, her eyes smoky with a passion he had aroused.

Sara broke off, startled, as he suddenly shoved his chair back from the table. "I've got to go check on the horses." Without another word, he was gone.

She blinked, wondering if it was something she'd said, or something about their being in this kitchen that caused him to make abrupt exits. First this morning and then just now he had abandoned her suddenly. With a sigh, she got to her feet and picked up the plates. He could be as rude as he liked, just as long as he found Cullen.

Maybe it was just his way to be brusque. He hadn't been any too gallant when he suggested that she might as well stay at the ranch tonight and offered her the use of a spare bedroom. She had the strange feeling that there was something about her he resented. Not just the situation in general, but something about her personally.

She had just finished drying the last of the dishes when the back of her neck began to tingle. She was almost getting used to his silent approaches and she turned calmly, her eyes meeting the hooded brilliance of his.

"I didn't want to snoop through the cupboards trying to find where things went, so I didn't put anything away."

"It wasn't necessary for you to do anything, but thank you."

They faced each other across the narrow expanse of buckling linoleum like warriors across a battlefield. Sara knew she was not just imagining the wary look in his eyes. Whatever his problem was, right now she didn't have the energy to struggle with it. Sleep had been elusive this last week, but she had the feeling that tonight she was going to sleep like a log. Knowing that something was being done to find Cullen lifted a huge weight from her shoulders.

"If you don't mind, I think I'll go to bed now. I really appreciate you letting me stay here. I wasn't looking forward to the drive back to civilization to find a motel."

"No problem. It gets cold this time of year, but there are plenty of blankets on the bed."

"Thank you." She stood next to the sink for a moment longer, reluctant to approach the door where he stood. As if sensing her thoughts he stepped out of the doorway, and Sara gave him a strained smile and moved forward.

With her attention on her host, she missed seeing the raised ridge of linoleum. The toe of her boot caught on it and she gave a startled gasp as she stumbled and pitched forward, hands flung out to break the inevitable fall.

An iron-hard bar caught her across the middle and she was spun upright and slammed into a hard wall of muscle. Her fingers closed on the soft fabric of a denim shirt and for a moment she could only stare dazedly at the solid blue barrier in front of her.

The first two buttons of his shirt were undone and she could see a light mat of dark curly hair against the warm coppery skin of his chest. Her quick breathing drew in a heated masculine scent that owed nothing to cologne. Just soap and man.

Reluctantly, she lifted her eyes to his face, almost afraid of what she would see. She wondered why she'd never realized that a fire could blaze green. His hands had come to rest on her hips, his long fingers on the swell of her buttocks, and now his fingers tightened, pulling her closer into the cradle of his thighs, pressing her breasts firmly against his chest.

Sara stopped breathing, her eyes never leaving the heated green of his. He was going to kiss her. She should move back, say something light to break the tension. She shouldn't just stand here, her fingers still locked on his shirt. His eyes shifted to her mouth and she forgot how to breathe. His head dipped slightly. Did she strain toward him?

As quickly as it had begun, it ended. His head came up, leaving her mouth feeling bereft. His hands slid away from her hips, and she wondered if she imagined the reluctance in the movement. She blinked and looked away from the brilliant depths of his eyes. It took a conscious effort for her to make her fingers release their grip on his shirt and her feet move.

She backed one step away and the heel of her boot caught on the same ridge that had been her downfall moments ago. Cody's hand flashed out and caught her elbow, steadying her. Even that small contact sent tingling waves of awareness up her arm.

She laughed shakily. "I guess I'm more tired than I thought."

His eyes followed her solemnly, their expression unreadable. "I'll have to fix that section of the floor."

She rubbed her hands up and down her thighs. "Well, I'll get to bed now. I'll watch where I walk a little more carefully."

He nodded. "Good night."

She could feel his eyes on her back until she turned the corner of the wide doorway, and even then she could still feel his presence. In the small bedroom he had given her, with the door safely shut behind her, Sara let her breath out in a long whoosh.

She was going to have to watch herself. She was vulnerable right now and Cody Wolf would be dynamite at the best of times. She undressed and tugged on a flannel nightshirt before crawling under the pile of covers and switching off the lamp.

She was immediately aware of silence. Not just quiet, but absolute stillness. No traffic noises, none of the vague rumble that seemed to be a constant companion even in the suburbs. Just quiet. A soft sound broke the stillness, reminding her that she was not alone. She stirred restlessly, remembering that moment when she had been pressed against the length of him.

The planes and angles of his face were vivid beneath her closed eyelids. If she drew a deep breath, she could almost imagine that his scent filled her nostrils. Her eyes widened onto pitch darkness. There were no city lights to ease the heavy blanket of night. A door snicked quietly shut somewhere nearby, and Sara was suddenly intensely aware of being all alone with a man she knew nothing about. She searched for some fear in the thought, but it wasn't there.

She felt as safe with Cody as she did with David. David! She had called him before leaving Denver this morning to tell him where she was going, and that was the last time she'd thought about him. He certainly hadn't been on her mind when she'd been practically glued to Cody Wolf earlier.

She owed David so much. He'd helped her start her career; he'd eased her through those first terrifying months of trying to hold everything together for Cullen, trying to make a home for the boy. She loved David. She hadn't given him a formal acceptance of his proposal yet, but they both knew that she was going to marry him. Of course she was going to marry him. But, then, why had she hesitated to commit herself to him and why did one touch from Cody Wolf set off fireworks she'd never felt with David?

David. She had to stop thinking about her enigmatic host and start thinking about her almost-fiancé. She tried to summon David's features, but they immediately wavered and blurred, to be replaced by a harder, more angular face with emerald eyes that looked as if they could see into her soul. Her head moved restlessly against the pillow, banishing the image and forcing David's more gentle features into focus. But they wavered, brown eyes shifting to green.

With a little sound that was almost a sob, Sara abandoned the effort. It was just that she was tired. Naturally Cody's features would be more clear. After all, right now he was very important to her. He was her means of finding Cullen. That was why his image kept overriding David's. It had nothing to do with the fact that when he touched her, her senses seemed to catch fire.

CODY TURNED RESTLESSLY, part of him fighting the urge to sleep. Sleeping meant dreaming and he wasn't sure he wanted to dream tonight. He had the feeling that Sara Grant was going to play all too prominent a role in his dreams. Her presence in his home made the old house feel alive in a way it hadn't been since his mother's death almost twenty years ago.

He sat up in bed, resting his elbows on his knees and staring across the dark room. He had a sudden urge for the cigarettes he had given up twelve years ago, and his mouth twisted in a half smile. He'd known her less than twenty-four hours and she was already giving him a nicotine fit. But it didn't feel like twenty-four hours.

Looking into those ever-changing eyes, he'd had the feeling he'd known her forever. That she'd been part of him since time began. That was a foolish idea, of course. It was just that he'd been shut away in these mountains for too many months with no one but Dancer to talk to.

Maybe after he'd found the wreck and the boy, dead or alive, he'd take a weekend and drive to Laramie or Cheyenne and get himself dead drunk, find a willing woman and give the locals a chance to shake their heads over Indians who couldn't hold their liquor.

He slid back down under the covers, resolved to sleep dreamlessly and banish thoughts of a fragile woman with a will of iron and eyes as changeable as a mountain sunset.

"WE'LL LEAVE this afternoon." Cody ran his fingers through his hair, casually tousling the already-shaggy style. "I've got to drive over to the Williams's place and ask their oldest boy to keep an eye on my place. Then I'll pack the horses with everything I'm likely to need. We should be ready to leave by early afternoon. Won't get very far before dark, but it'll be a start."

Sara sipped her coffee. "How do you plan to go about finding the crash? Search and rescue didn't have much luck. And why horses? Wouldn't it be better to rent a chopper or a plane or something?"

"If you wanted a high-tech search you came to the wrong place. Didn't Larkin tell you that I have to beat a tom-tom and dance around a fire to find the crash sites?"

There was a wealth of bitterness in his words, and Sara blinked uncertainly. "Well, actually, John didn't tell me much of anything. But I don't care what you do as long as you find Cullen."

Cody turned away from her to pour a cup of coffee, shaken by his reaction to her perfectly natural question. He'd thought the old wounds were long healed, but something about her seemed to bring all the bitterness rushing to the surface. He turned back, forcing his mouth into a tight smile.

"Larkin and I did not get along too well," he offered by way of both explanation and apology. "I'm using horses because that's the way I work. If the wreck could be found from the air, you wouldn't have come to me."

"Fair enough," Sara agreed easily, forgetting that he had answered only a part of her question. "While you make the arrangements, I'll sort out the things I'll need. Do you have some kind of a pack I can put stuff in?"

"A pack for what?" he asked blankly, afraid he already knew the answer.

"Clothes, mostly. I brought plenty of jeans and I think I've got enough sweaters. I don't know if my coat is—"

"Wait a minute." He waited until she looked at him, her brows raised in question. "You're not going with me. You can stay here, but you'd probably be more comfortable staying in a motel somewhere. You can leave word with Bob Williams of where you'll be and I'll contact you as soon as I get back."

"That's very considerate of you but I'd planned on going along."

His tone matched hers for reasonability. "You'll have to change plans. I'm not taking you with me."

"I can understand why you'd have some doubts, but I—"

"I don't have any doubts at all," he interrupted, letting her hear the steel in his voice. "You're not going."

She stopped trying to argue reasonably.

"I'm going with you."

"Like hell you are!"

"Like hell I'm not!" Sara's chin set stubbornly and her eyes didn't waver from the angry green of his.

"I'm not taking you with me!"

"I'm going, whether you like it or not!"

Cody slammed his coffee cup down on the counter and took two angry strides forward, resting his palms on the edge of the table and leaning toward her menacingly. Sara lifted her chin and met him glare for glare.

"I am not taking a woman who doesn't know one end of a horse from another on a mountain trip of unknown duration."

"Cullen is my family. I'm going with you to find him. And, as a matter of fact, I do know which end of a horse is which, and I know which end I'd label you."

He jerked upright, his brows coming down in menacing black hooks over eyes that burned with irritation. "All right, lady. You're welcome to come along if you can prove to me that you're not going to be a liability. This is no jaunt in the park, and I'm damned if I'll risk my neck looking for your nephew and trying to look after a damned model who's afraid to break a fingernail at the same time."

Sara stood, wishing she didn't have to look up so far to meet his eyes. "You can be damned all you like. I'm going with you. If I thought I was going to be a liability, I wouldn't go. I can ride and I've done a fair amount of camping. I don't expect hot and cold running water and maid service on the side of a mountain and I am not afraid of breaking a fingernail. If I can't keep up, you can feel free to leave me, and I'll find my own way home."

"You'll pull your own weight from start to finish," he warned.

"I wouldn't have it any other way."

He glared at her in frustration a moment longer and then muttered something unprintable under his breath before spinning away. He picked up his mug and downed the last of his coffee. From the way his hand wrapped around the thick porcelain, she had the feeling that he was wishing it was her neck. But if he was inclined to violence, he restrained the urge.

He picked up his hat from the counter and jammed it on his head. "I'll be back in two hours. Have your things sorted and ready to pack."

Sara resisted the urge to stick her tongue out at his back as he left. It was probably a good thing he wasn't wearing the traditional cowboy boots. The heels would have gouged holes in the floor. Even in soft moccasins he managed to stomp.

Cody put the truck into gear and reversed into a gravel-spinning turn before slamming the transmission into forward and heading up the hill. She was the most irritatingly stubborn woman he had ever run across. He couldn't remember the last time he'd let someone get him so angry, and she'd done it effortlessly.

He was half-tempted to tell her to take her money, her nephew and her pigheadedness and get off his ranch. But he'd had the dream again last night, more vivid, more detailed. And when he awoke, he found he shared her conviction that the boy was alive. The other times there had been only death in the dreams, but this time he sensed something more.

No, no matter how angry she made him and no matter how badly he wanted her out of his life, he couldn't back out now. For better or worse, he had to see this thing through to the finish.

Chapter Four

"I don't see why you have to go through my clothing." Sara's voice was nothing short of belligerent and Cody had to grit his teeth to resist the urge to grab her and shake her. The only thing that stopped him was the knowledge that, in her shoes, he wouldn't like the idea of a stranger handling his personal belongings.

"I'm not going to go through your things. I have to pack them. No, you can't do it yourself." He cut off the protest he could see forming. "You may have done some camping, but I sincerely doubt that you've had any experience packing a horse for a trip into the mountains. The load has to be carefully balanced or it's hard on the animals."

He paused to let that sink in and then added one final statement. "My animals—I pack them."

Sara swallowed and nodded without meeting his eyes. She didn't know why she'd argued anyway. What did it matter who packed the stuff? It was only clothing. But the thought of those long, tanned fingers among the delicate satins and lace of her underwear brought a strange tightness to her chest.

"You're right, of course. Everything is stacked on my bed. Shall I bring it down to the corral?"

Gracious in defeat, Cody thought savagely. With each new facet that he saw in Sara Grant, she seemed more and more dangerous.

"No. I'll come back up for it when I'm ready."

What had sent him off this time? Sara winced as the screen door slammed shut behind him. She'd backed down, hadn't she? Wasn't that what he'd wanted? She turned away from the door without an answer. All that really mattered here was finding Cullen. Everything else was secondary. If Cody Wolf wanted to snap and snarl from here to the Continental Divide, it didn't matter to her.

She went into the bedroom to look over the neat stacks of clothing once more, trying to make sure that she had everything she was likely to need. Her only concern was that her coat might not be heavy enough, but it would have to do. She could always layer a sweater or two under it.

She crossed the room and leaned against the wall next to the window, looking up at the mountains that loomed over the valley. The valley floor was filled with sunshine and the temperature barely required long sleeves, but it would be much colder up there. She hugged herself unconsciously, trying not to think of just how cold it might be.

A floorboard creaked behind her and she spun around. Cody stood in the doorway. Sara stared at him for a silent moment, trying to conceal the shiver that ran up her spine when her eyes met the brilliance of his. He stepped into the room, and it was as if the air had acquired an electric charge.

If he felt the same awareness that was stealing her breath away, he gave no sign of it. His eyes skimmed over her impassively as he crossed the room to stand next to the bed. He was only a few feet away. If she stretched out her arm, she could almost touch him. Sara's fingers clenched into fists against her sides. She didn't want to touch him. She refused to want to touch him.

His hand came up and she held her breath. Was he going to reach out? She was alone with him, miles from another human being. She would be helpless to stop him if he chose to use his strength against her.

But the emotion that quickened her pulse wasn't fear. She trusted this lean stranger. She was trusting him with her life and Cullen's. No, she wasn't afraid. But she wasn't quite ready to put a name to what she did feel.

His fingers closed around a leather strap that crossed his shoulder, and Sara only then realized that he was carrying a pair of worn leather saddlebags. He tossed them on the bed next to her neat stacks of clothing.

"You can use these to pack some of your things in." If he felt that he was compromising, not a hint of it showed in his husky voice. "Just be sure to balance the load as much as possible . . . and let me pack anything bulky on the packhorses."

It took a moment for Sara to realize what he was saying. He was offering her privacy, as much as was possible. Her smile was a bit shaky around the edges and her eyes were a little too bright as she thanked him.

"Thank you. I really appreciate this. Is there anything I can do to help?"

Cody's eyes skimmed over the delicate contours of her face and, for a moment, Sara thought she saw a softening. But it must have been her imagination.

"The only thing you could do to help would be to agree to stay here, and I don't think you're going to do that."

Sara's spine stiffened. "I'm coming with you."

"So you've said. Pack up the saddlebags and be down at the corral in an hour. I'll introduce you to your horse and you can saddle her."

"Fine." She all but spit the word at him. Her fingers itched to strike him. He was the most obnoxious, nasty, irritating man she'd ever met.

As if he could read her thoughts, he raised one black brow in a silently sardonic comment before he turned and left the room, his moccasins silent on the scuffed floors. Sara watched him go, mentally calling him every name she could think of. She had no choice but to tolerate him. If it meant finding Cullen, she'd put up with Lucifer himself, but she didn't have to like it. The electricity that seemed to course between them was obviously pure dislike.

CODY STALKED TO THE BARN, his strides eating up the distance with angry speed. He should have just refused to take her along. He should have put his foot down and just flat out told her that she was not going with him.

He swung into the barn and crossed to Dancer's stall. The bay nodded a greeting, his nose prodding demandingly against Cody's breast pocket. As always happened when he was around horses, Cody found he couldn't sustain his anger. He smiled softly, murmuring a greeting to the big stallion.

"I should have put my foot down." He took something from his pocket and opened his palm flat, letting Dancer snuffle eagerly at the sugar cube that lay there. His free hand stroked the horse's muscled neck. "Why is it that I have a feeling if I'd put my foot down, she'd bite it off?" Dancer snorted a reply and butted his head on Cody's shoulder. Absently, Cody scratched behind the horse's ear. "And why do I have the feeling that I'd be very disappointed if she did agree to stay?"

When he'd seen her standing beside that window, looking up at the mountains, he'd known what she was thinking as surely as if he had read her mind. It would be colder up there. How would her nephew cope? A surprising emotion had swept over him. He'd wanted to put his arms around her and tell her that everything was going to be all right. It was an urge he'd never felt toward a woman and he didn't want to feel it now.

With a muttered curse, he gave Dancer one last scratch and backed away from the stall. He was aware of the dangers this woman represented and he'd just have to make sure that she didn't disrupt his life any more than could be helped. He'd go look for her nephew because it was something he had to do. Something was drawing him toward the crash and he had to follow that pull, but that was as far as it went.

Once they'd found the boy, she would leave him to go back to the life he was carefully building, and he'd never have to see her again, which was exactly what he wanted.

Wasn't it?

No matter how much he wished her out of his life, Cody had to admit that Sara Grant had a gutsiness that he couldn't help but admire. She hadn't backed down from him this morning and she wasn't showing any signs of backing down now.

Even now, the angle of her chin dared him to say anything the least bit derogatory. He watched her without seeming to, his eyes shadowed by the brim of his hat. His hands moved automatically through the motions of loading the pack animals. He'd done it so often that it didn't take much conscious thought to balance the packs carefully, making sure that neither animal carried too much weight.

Most of his attention was on the woman a few feet away. She'd presented herself at the corral precisely an hour after he'd left her in the house. The saddlebags were clutched in her hands, and he'd noticed with approval that she hadn't overpacked. He said nothing, however. Instead, he introduced her to the horse he'd selected for her to ride.

"This is Satin. She's gentle and one of the best trail animals I've seen. There's your saddle. Take some time to get to know her and then saddle up. I'm leaving in half an hour."

His tone made it clear that he was leaving in half an hour, and if she wasn't ready to go, he wouldn't be waiting. Sara glared after him as he walked away. Irritating man. She turned back to the horse and met a pair of soft brown eyes that seemed to sympathize with her feelings. Satin was a palomino, the color of a new gold coin, with a silvery white mane and tail and the biggest, most expressive eyes Sara had ever seen.

"Oh, what a beauty you are." She breathed the words, absently groping in her pocket for the sugar cube she'd filched from the kitchen. She had no idea whether or not Cody fed his horses sugar, but one wouldn't hurt and it could go a long way toward making friends with her mount.

Satin snuffled the sugar cube up without a moment's hesitation, crunching it between strong teeth while Sara ran her palm along the horse's gleaming neck. The irritation she felt toward her reluctant host disappeared as she talked quietly with the horse. With Cody's departure time firmly set in her mind, she couldn't spend as long with Satin as she would have liked, but by the time she started to saddle the mare, Sara felt confident that they'd reached a pretty firm understanding.

The saddling operation went smoothly until it came time to actually lift the saddle up onto the mare's back. When Sara told Cody that she knew horses, it had been a bit of an exaggeration. Her brother, Evan, had known his way around horses, and Cullen loved them. Sara had done some riding and she knew how to saddle a horse, but she was by no means an expert. The sheer weight of the saddle almost defeated her.

Luckily, Satin turned out to be the most patient of creatures, and Cody, apparently engrossed in putting the finishing touches to the packhorses, didn't seem to notice her struggles. Sara promised herself if he offered to help, or made some smug comment about her being a helpless female, she'd slug him one.

Satin stood rock steady even when the saddle bumped into her flank, and with a burst of strength, Sara managed to get the heavy leather up onto the horse's back. She leaned against Satin's side for a moment, willing strength back into her shaking arms.

Cody watched her from under the brim of his hat. He would have offered to help her with the saddle but he had the feeling that she'd have shoved the offer back in his teeth. She was no expert but she got the job done. She cinched the saddle snug and then turned to look at him. Her expression was so full of triumph that he almost smiled. But he didn't want to smile at her. He didn't want to like her.

He crossed to her side, silently checking the tightness of the cinch, and Sara watched him through narrowed eyes. The horse was perfectly saddled. She wasn't an expert but she knew there was nothing wrong with the job she'd done. If he said just one word...

"Looks good. I've got everything packed. You won't need a coat right now, but I'm going to tie it to the back of your saddle. Most likely you'll need it before we stop for the night."

Sara watched as he secured the coat, trying not to outwardly acknowledge the warm glow his approval brought to her body. It was just that she felt good about showing him that she wasn't helpless—that's all it was.

Twenty minutes later she boosted herself into the saddle and turned Satin's head to follow Cody's lead. A red-headed eighteen-year-old with a slightly gap-toothed grin waved from the end of the corral, and Sara lifted her hand in acknowledgment. In Billy Williams's pocket was a brief letter to David letting him know what was happening. She only hoped the boy didn't forget to take it into town and mail it.

If Cody was leaving him in charge of his stock, then the boy must be more responsible than his freckled face seemed to indicate. Funny, how she had such confidence in Cody's judgment. She might not like him, but her instincts insisted that she believe in him.

She lifted her face to the mountains ahead of them, inhaling deeply. The air was so crisp and clean she could almost taste it. A far cry from the L.A. smog.

In front of her, Cody sat on the bay horse as if he and the animal were one. His back was straight but not rigid, and he swayed easily in rhythm with the horse's pace. The two packhorses followed Dancer, their heads up, ears pricked forward as if in anticipation of the trail ahead. Satin brought up the rear, her pace smooth and easy.

Ranging a few yards ahead of Dancer was an animal that Cody had introduced simply as Dog. In Sara's opinion, this was a definite misnomer. There was nothing in the least doglike about the huge black and white creature. He had loped around the side of the barn, scaring her half out of her wits.

When introduced, Sara had held out her hand, but Dog had disdained anything so common as a sniff. He'd looked at her out of yellow eyes that held an almost-human intelligence, and Sara had the feeling that she'd been weighed and filed. She only hoped she'd been filed in a category of friendly acquaintances. She didn't think she'd like being on the wrong side of Dog. Cody had murmured a few words to the beast, and Dog had taken up his position at the head of their little caravan.

From her position at the tail end of the expedition, Sara had a clear view of the picture they presented. The ranch lay behind them, its few reminders of civilization out of sight. Ahead of them lay the mountains, fundamentally unchanged since Zebulon Pike first saw them a hundred and seventy-five years before.

Sara didn't even have to close her eyes to imagine herself in a much earlier time. Cody's jeans and denim shirt blended easily with that image. The rifle that rested against his saddle might be more sophisticated than the ones the explorers had carried, but its purpose hadn't changed.

Falling into the rhythm of the horse's movements, she let her mind drift. They were a husband and wife journeying toward their new home. Perhaps up ahead lay a secluded valley where they would settle. Cody would fell logs for a cabin—only one room, but there were just the two of them. They'd have to hurry because winter was almost here. There'd be game in the mountains and in the spring she'd plant a garden. But between now and then there was a long, cold winter to get through.

Months with no one to rely on but each other. Her man would have to spend time hunting, and it would be hard to stretch their supplies until spring. But it would be worth it, because to offset the long hours of work, there would be the long, dark hours of night when there were just the two of them. He'd come to her in the flickering firelight, his body lean and hard. Her breasts would swell to his touch, her...

Sara snapped her eyes open, aware of a heavy feeling low in her belly. The air felt cold against the fiery heat in her cheeks. Thank God no one could see her face. Her thoughts must be written in scarlet letters across her forehead. It was one thing to daydream idly about what it would be like to live in another time. It was something else altogether when her fantasies took on a life of their own. She hunched her arms together, vividly aware of the way her nipples had puckered into taut peaks.

Her gloved hands tightened on the reins, loosening when Satin tossed her head in protest. Sara leaned forward, murmuring apologies to the mare. When she sat upright again, her cheeks were cool and she had her thoughts under control again. Cody Wolf was an attractive man. She could acknowledge that without becoming too aware of it. Right now she was forced to depend on him, both for herself and Cullen. She had to remember that she was in an emotionally volatile state. That's all it was. Her feelings didn't really have anything to do with the man who sat on his horse so gracefully only a few yards in front of her.

Cody glanced back over his shoulder, wondering what it was that had brought such a stern look to Sara's delicate features. He swung around in the saddle, facing forward again, but her face stayed with him as if painted on a gossamer curtain between him and the mountains.

BY THE TIME Cody drew Dancer to a halt and the rest of the horses stopped behind him, Sara felt as if she'd been in the saddle for weeks instead of hours. Her spine ached, her legs seemed permanently bowed around the barrel of her horse and she couldn't even bear to contemplate the condition of her buttocks. Cody dismounted with an ease that made her want to hit him, preferably with a large rock.

She eased her leg over the saddle and managed to land on the ground with absolutely no grace, but she didn't really care. All that mattered was the feel of solid earth under her boots. Her knees quivered and threatened to collapse beneath her, and she clung to the saddle until they steadied enough to hold her upright. She looked at Satin and bit her lip to stifle a wave of despair. The first rule was to take care of your animal. Evan had drummed that into her every time they went riding. The problem was, she couldn't possibly lift the saddle off. If it had been heavy before, it was going to weigh twice as much now.

But she was damned if she was going to ask Mr. Friendly for help. Gritting her teeth, she reached for the cinch strap, only to find other hands there first.

"Go sit down." His husky voice was brusque, and some of Sara's exhaustion vanished beneath a surge of pride.

"I can do it. I rode her, I'll take care of her," she insisted.

His hands stilled on the cinch and he turned to look at her. Those brilliant green eyes swept over her from the tousled ponytail that held her hair off her face, down over the green plaid shirt and snug denims to her black boots. Sara had the feeling that he could see every aching muscle, including her shaking knees.

He let the silence stretch a moment before his eyes met hers again. "I don't want to waste time arguing with you. You're dead on your feet. Go sit down."

"But..."

His jaw hardened and Sara gave up the argument. She turned away, holding her back rigidly straight. Damn him! Damn him for seeing her weakness and not even having the decency to pretend he didn't. It was some time before she cooled off enough to pay any attention to their surroundings. For the last half an hour, she'd been riding in a fog.

Their camp lay in a narrow valley that boasted a small stream trickling through the middle of it. The streambed was much wider than the shallow flow of water, and it wasn't hard to guess that when the snow melted in the high country in spring the delicate trickle would become a modest river. The grass was still green, contrasting with the darker color of the blue spruce that crept down the sides of the mountains around them.

The setting was like a painting of the Old West, with nothing to disturb its picture-book perfection. Cody fit right into the picture as he worked around the horses, unloading packs and picketing the animals in the autumn grasses. He'd set his hat aside, and a light breeze teased playfully at his thick hair.

Sara leaned back on her hands, stretching her sore legs out in front of her. The sun was sinking rapidly behind the mountains. It would be totally dark soon. Her first night in the wilderness. Staring up the mountain, she wondered how many more nights she'd have to spend here before they found the crash site.

How many people had been in this valley before them? Had a band of hardy pioneers camped here once? Indians? The Indians who had lived in this area must surely have known of this exquisite little valley. She focused hazily on her reluctant guide. He'd said something about beating on a tom-tom and dancing around fires. Was he a Native American? Perhaps his ancestors had once lived in this valley.

Cody stood next to Dancer, rubbing a curry brush over the stallion's back. There was a softness in his face that she hadn't seen before, and it was obvious that he loved the horse. If she narrowed her eyes, it wasn't hard to picture him without the jeans and shirt, the long moccasins clinging to his calves and a deerskin breechclout his only other covering. His legs would be muscled and...

"Wake up. Supper's ready." Sara awoke with a start. She was disoriented to find herself lying on the ground, a light blanket thrown over her body. The sun was completely gone and the temperature had dropped to a chilly level.

Cody was crouched beside her, only withdrawing his hand from her shoulder when he saw that her eyes were staying open. Sara sat up and rubbed her eyes like a sleepy child.

"What time is it?"

"It's after dark." And that answer was enough. The artificial division of days into hours and minutes was not relevant once civilization was left behind. All that really mattered was that the sun was gone.

"Have I been asleep long?"

"Not long." She looked so soft and feminine just waking from her nap that Cody had to fight the urge to brush the tendrils of hair back from her forehead and kiss the sleep from her eyes. He stood up, backing away from temptation.

"If you want to wash up in the stream before dinner, I suggest you get a move on. We want to get dinner out of the way so we can get an early start in the morning."

Sara was still groping through the sleepy fog that clouded her mind when he walked away. Ten minutes later, she sat on a small camp stool and dug into the hot stew Cody had dished onto her plate. The crisp air and the afternoon's ride had left her with an appetite, and food had never tasted better.

"This is the stew we had last night, isn't it?"

"Seemed a shame to throw it out. Billy will drive home for supper most nights." His eyes swept over her. "Enjoy it while you can. After tonight, we'll be eating canned and dried foods."

Sara shrugged, dipping a slightly squashed slice of bread into the rich gravy. "I don't mind." If he was trying to make her regret coming along, he was going to have to come up with a more powerful threat than boring food.

Cody refused her offer of help with the cleanup, insisting brusquely that he worked better alone. Sara had no idea whether he was being kind to her stiff muscles or not, but she accepted his refusal. The air had grown chilly enough that she'd dug her jacket out of the pack he'd dropped beside her, and now she was grateful for its warmth as she huddled next to the fire.

She reached out to add a stick of wood to the leaping flames and then jerked her hand back as a dark shape loomed up from the darkness outside the circle of light. Her first thought was *Wolf!* and the breath she drew in was intended for a scream that died unvoiced when she recognized Dog. She'd lost track of the animal as the afternoon wore on. He'd disappeared ahead, and she hadn't seen him since they made camp. Now, looming up out of the darkness, the shaggy body looked bigger than ever and the black patch that surrounded one yellow eye gave him a sinister look that made a shiver run up Sara's spine.

Cody was somewhere out in the darkness. She had no idea where or how far away. It was just her and the dog. She cleared her throat, remembering her brother's admonitions that animals could sense fear. But surely this creature realized he was too big to inspire anything but fear.

"Hi, Dog."

Those golden eyes studied her for a long, unblinking moment, and Sara hoped he wasn't considering the digestibility of her nylon jacket. He seemed to come to some decision, because he padded around the fire toward her. Sara forgot how to breathe. Dog could probably tear her throat out long before Cody could do anything to save her, assuming that Cody wouldn't welcome his dog's solution to the problem she represented.

The beast stopped in front of her, and some instinct made her hold out her hand, even while her mind screamed that she might as well hold out a ham sandwich. There was a moment when she felt the damp warmth of the dog's breath on her fingers, and then he turned and lay down next to her, facing the fire.

Sara pulled her hand back and tucked it under her other arm, though the chill she felt had little to do with the cold air. She turned her head to look at the animal, wondering if she was expected to pet him. But there was a limit to her courage and she decided to leave well enough alone.

Cody stepped silently into the firelight, taking in the picture they made, the huge dog and the slender woman. His brows rose. It wasn't often that Dog accepted a human into his small circle of acquaintances.

Sara looked up, her smile slightly shaky. "Is his name really Dog?"

Cody set the load of firewood down within reach of where he'd unroll his sleeping bag.

"That's right."

"Dog?" She laughed. "Well, it has a certain appealing honesty to it."

Her laugh sent a shiver through him, and Cody found himself smiling.

"Spot didn't seem quite right."

Sara blinked. He'd actually addressed a friendly remark toward her. In fact, she didn't think it would be going too far to say that there'd been a hint of humor in the words.

"I would have thought Horse might have worked." She wanted to encourage this fragile rapport.

"He wasn't quite that large when he was a puppy." He fed a few sticks of wood into the fire.

Sara shivered, drawing a bit closer to the fire. From under his lashes, Cody watched her. The firelight danced over the smooth perfection of her skin, casting enticing shadows and highlights. She glanced up at the mountains and shivered.

"It must be a lot colder up there." It didn't take a mind reader to know where her thoughts lay.

Compassion stirred in him. She was thinking about the boy, wondering what he was doing, if he was cold or injured. There was nothing he could say to reassure her. He wanted to put his arms around her and ease the frightened look on her face. He wanted to tell her everything was going to be all right. But he couldn't do that.

He reached into his pack and pulled out a silver flask. He lifted it questioningly. "Cognac? It helps to take the chill out of the air."

She shook her head and then watched as he poured himself a fingerful, sipping it slowly. More contrasts. Sitting beside a campfire in the wilds of the Rocky Mountains with a man who looked like someone from a page out of history—and he was drinking cognac. It should be rotgut whiskey.

"Tomorrow night I'll set up the tent, but tonight we'll sleep without it."

Twenty minutes later she snuggled deep into the warmth of the sleeping bag Cody had brought for her. Across the fire Cody lay quietly, and she wondered if he'd already fallen asleep. Along the side of her that faced away from the fire, Dog had stretched himself out, providing her with a warm bulwark against the chill night.

It was very quiet. Only the crackling of the fire and the almost-silent murmur of the stream broke the absolute stillness in the little valley. The soft hoot of an owl seemed an appropriate lullaby. Not too far away, a coyote howled mournfully, his cry echoing off the mountains. Sara shivered. The sound drew an atavistic response from her, as if a race memory drawn from prehistory told her that the predator's howl could mean death.

Opening her eyes, she stared up at the sky. There were so many stars, more than could be counted in a hundred lifetimes. She'd lived so long in Los Angeles that she'd forgotten the night sky could look like this. No smog, no city lights to dim the glory. Just a blanket of sparkling lights.

The coyote howled again and she clenched her teeth. Where was Cullen? Could he hear that lonesome sound? Was he safe?

"The Comanche looked on the coyote as a brother."

Cody's voice was quiet, husky. He didn't seem to expect a response from her and Sara didn't offer one.

"He was called the Trickster. There are many legends about him. Every tribe had stories of the coyote's cleverness. The Zuni believed that he stole the sun and the moon from the Kachinas. They were kept in a box and he helped the eagle steal the box, but then he could not resist the urge to peak into the box and the sun and moon escaped."

His voice was low, almost singsong, and Sara found her eyes drifting shut. Along her side, Dog shifted and moaned in his sleep. The fire cast dancing shadows across her eyelids.

"And there are stories of how he placed the stars in the sky. So many stories, it's impossible to know them all."

Cody paused, listening to her quiet breathing. He didn't have to see her to know that she slept. He could hear it in the shallow rhythm of her breaths. He shifted restlessly inside the sleeping bag. He should go to sleep, but in sleep lay dreams.

He was no longer sure which he feared most, dreams of the crash or dreams of ever-changing eyes. He stared up at the mountains' dark shapes against the star-bright sky. Was the boy up there, alive and struggling to survive, or was Cody leading Sara toward a scene of death and destruction?

He shook his head. Whatever was up there, he had no choice but to take this trip. Fate, or the gods, or whatever deity, chose to interest itself in his life. It was no longer a matter of choosing to look for the crash site. It was something he had to do.

The Survivor

CULLEN PLACED the last stone and stood back to look at his handiwork. Crude but functional. A huge arrow pointed in the direction he would take in the morning. Anyone who found the crash would know that there had been a survivor, and this would tell them where he had headed.

He turned and limped back to the shelter of the demolished aircraft, lowering himself clumsily onto his sleeping bag. The light was fading fast and he worked quickly, crumbling bits of bark into the ashes of the day's fire and blowing on it until they caught. He added twigs and bigger pieces of bark until the little fire began to crackle, and then he carefully set a few small branches in the flames. He had matches, but he didn't know how long they might have to last and he was conserving them along with everything else he had.

He and Bill had been on their way back from a camping trip and their supplies were low. Enough to get him on his way, but he was going to have to supplement his food with what he could find in the wild.

Five days since the crash. He set a pot to heat over the fire and searched for a bag of dried soup. His injured knee had gone past the point of pain and had settled into a dull throbbing that beat in time to his pulse. If he was lucky, he might not lose full use of the joint. But then his luck had been a little dicey lately.

He dumped the soup mix into the steaming water and set a lid over the top of it to let it steep. He'd realized today that he wasn't going to be able to wait calmly by the wreckage until someone found it. It had snowed again yesterday. It wouldn't be too long before the snow deepened and winter set in with a vengeance.

He couldn't stay here much longer. He cocked his head as a coyote's howl echoed eerily across the mountain. Unconsciously, his hand went to the pistol strapped to his side. A coyote would probably prefer to avoid a man if possible, but he wasn't in any position to outrun anything. With his leg the way it was, he would be fair game for any predator.

He picked up a spoon and lifted the steaming pan of soup to begin his supper. Tomorrow morning, he would start walking down the mountain. With a compass and a map and some common sense, he should be able to make it. If his leg would hold up. And that was a big if.

Chapter Five

When Sara woke the next morning, she found that the
only thing worse than riding a horse all day was waking up the next morning. Every muscle in her body
protested vociferously when she tried to move. With an
effort she managed to sit upright, sure that the creak-
ing of her bones could be heard for miles around.

Cody was not in sight, for which she was thankful.
At least there were no witnesses to her painful struggle
to get out of her sleeping bag. The horses grazed
peacefully not far from the stream, but there was no
sign of her guide. Sara didn't care where he was. All she
cared about was that she had some privacy. She didn't
want to think about how ridiculous she must look on
her hands and knees, with her rear end thrust into the
air as she pushed herself upright.

Once she was more-or-less vertical, she was almost
brought down again when her feet tangled in her
sleeping bag. She groaned as she stumbled free of its
entangling folds, jarring muscles she hadn't even
known she had. She was dying. That was all there was
to it. No one could possibly be in this much pain and
survive.

There was a battered tin coffeepot on the rocks that surrounded the remains of last night's fire, and she looked at it longingly, wondering if she would end up falling headfirst into the ashes if she tried to bend over. With a sigh, she decided not to try it until her muscles had loosened up a bit. A walk seemed to be just the prescription. Wherever Cody had gone, she wanted to be ready to greet him when he returned. She didn't want him to see her hobbling around like the Hunchback of Notre Dame. That would just serve to confirm all the objections he had had to taking her along on this trip.

She looked at her boots, set neatly beside her sleeping bag, and then she looked at a small outcropping of rock that thrust up in the middle of the narrow valley. Between the two lay an expanse of slightly browned grass. Would the world come to an end if she walked that far barefoot? She bit her lip. The thought of struggling into her boots was not appealing. She was wearing heavy socks, which should be enough to protect her feet from any stray pebbles.

She stepped out gingerly, her walk a far cry from her normally graceful stride. At first it was all she could do to keep from moaning aloud at the pain in her legs. She was sure that there must be black-and-blue marks all over her aching body, and she was glad she'd slept in her clothes so that she didn't actually have to look at the bruises.

She'd taken only a few shuffling steps when she glimpsed a movement out of the corner of her eye. Immediately, she straightened her back and turned with what she hoped was a casual air. She wasn't going to let Cody see how badly she was hurting. It might give him an excuse to try and send her back to his ranch. The stiffness left her spine when she saw Dog loping toward her.

"Good morning." She held out her palm in greeting, and this time he deigned to sniff it. "Where's our friendly guide, huh?" She glanced around but there was still no sign of Cody. "I don't think he's very far away. I'm a little surprised he didn't want to get started before daylight."

Dog didn't have an answer to any of this. In fact, he didn't seem to have any real interest in the question of where Cody was, but Sara decided that was probably because he already knew where the man had gone. She shook her head. She didn't care where Cody was, just as long as he wasn't watching her first fumbling footsteps.

The walk to the rocks took longer than she'd expected, but by the time she got there, her legs seemed to be functioning less stiffly. She'd even managed to touch her knees once. Of course, she'd been aiming for her toes, but she'd settle for whatever she could get. Dog paced alongside her, seemingly unconcerned with her erratic progress. He listened to her muttered curses and prayers without comment.

Once at her goal, Sara stopped and twisted her body, gently coaxing more and more of her muscles back to life. The early morning sunshine was clean and pure and she found herself breathing deeply, almost tasting the air. The sunshine spilled over her, warming her, filling her with hope, and she stretched her arms upward as if to embrace its light.

When the world looked this clean and beautiful, it was impossible to believe that anything could be seriously wrong. For just this moment, she knew that Cullen and Bill were all right; Cody would find the plane and get them all down out of the mountains safely. She arched her back, smiling at everything and nothing.

She looked at the huge animal who sat patiently next to her. "You know, we really should work on a new name for you. Dog just doesn't have any real ring to it. You need something imposing to match your stature. What do you think of Caesar? Tsar? King is too common. What we need is something with real punch."

Dog hadn't expressed his opinion of any of her suggestions by so much as a twitch of an ear. He might not even have been aware of her presence for all the attention he seemed to be paying her. Sara didn't care. She wanted to hang on to this moment just a little while longer. In a minute she'd go back to the fire and pour herself a cup of coffee and eat whatever it was that Cody had planned for breakfast, and then she'd have to face getting back up on a horse and the reality of their search. But for just a moment more, she was going to pretend that the world was as perfect as it looked.

"How about Wapiti? That's an elk, and you're certainly close enough in size. Or we could go for Rhino. Now there's a name with impact. You like that?"

Dog had risen to his feet, the first reaction she'd seen. But it wasn't in response to her facetious suggestions for changing his name. Sara's smile faded as she took in his tense stance. A low growl rumbled up out of his throat, the first sound she'd heard him make. It was echoed by a lighter but far more ominous sound.

Sara felt as if her heart had stopped beating. Her entire body seemed frozen, and it was only with an effort that she forced her head to turn ever so slowly until she could look at the rocky outcropping.

Dog growled again, and again he was echoed by a dry, rusty-sounding rattle. She didn't really have to see the source of that sound. Coiled up not two feet from her legs, its triangular head weaving slightly, was a diamondback rattlesnake. Now the question was, just how far could he strike?

CODY ROSE TO HIS FEET with easy grace. On the nylon fishing line in his hand, two trout gleamed wetly in the early morning sun. If he'd been traveling alone, he would have been on the trail an hour ago. But he wasn't traveling alone and, for all her determination, he knew that Sara couldn't travel at the pace he could. He laid the trout in a shallow basket and then turned to face the morning sun.

He closed his eyes, letting the warm rays beat down on his face, driving away the chill of a nearly sleepless night. No, not sleepless. He'd slept, but he'd dreamed, too. And he'd awakened from those dreams more tired than before he'd slept. Always the mass of twisted metal. Sometimes there were bodies lying nearby, but he knew that those were the other crashes, the people he'd been too late to help.

He turned slightly, his nostrils flaring as if he could smell the trail they were following. He was being drawn to this crash strongly, as if he were tied to it with a piece of leather thong that was gradually shrinking, pulling him closer whether he willed it or not. The pull was so strong he had to believe it was because this time he wouldn't be too late—he had to believe that.

And always in the dreams were Sara's eyes—sometimes the blue of a mountain sky, sometimes the purple of a columbine. He felt as if he could fall into those eyes and drown in the promise they seemed to hold out.

He shook his head and opened his eyes. There was a danger in seeing too much in the dreams. Naturally, she would be in the dreams. She was the driving force behind this trip, which was the only reason she haunted him.

It had nothing to do with the silky length of her dark lashes, or with the way her hair seemed to be made of sunshine. The satin of her skin had no bearing on the matter, and the gentle curves of her body didn't make him long to feel that softness against his own much-harder frame. They had a business arrangement, nothing more.

He couldn't afford to believe anything else. If he started building fantasies around her, he was doomed to disappoint. They were worlds apart, in more ways than one. The only tie between them was the aircraft that lay somewhere above.

He bent to pick up the fish but stiffened before his hand touched the basket. The feeling of danger was so sharp it was almost a pain in his head. His fingers went to the knife that lay sheathed against his calf. With the haft in his palm, he spun around, blade up, ready to face whatever threatened. But there was nothing, just the quiet waters of the stream.

The feeling of danger persisted, and without conscious thought he slid the knife back into its sheath and began to run. The soft suede soles of his moccasins were silent on the grass. The closer he got to the camp, the more urgent the feeling of danger became. He'd left Dog with Sara. There wasn't much that could threaten her that he couldn't scare off. Besides, most wild animals would avoid the scent of man if given a chance.

He jumped, tucking his feet up under his body, taking a boulder in a leap that had all the grace of a deer.

He swung around a bend in the stream and there was Sara.

She was standing in front of a rock outcropping, Dog at her side. Cody skidded to a halt next to the remains of last night's fire, stopping only long enough to grab his rifle. He didn't have to hear the dusty rattle to know what held the woman and the dog frozen.

SARA FELT as if she had turned to stone. Every bone in her body was rigid, every muscle frozen into place. She couldn't even move her eyes away from that flattened triangle of a head and the two tiny eyes that seemed to watch her with so much malevolence. Beside her, Dog was utterly still, only the occasional growl that rumbled out of his throat told her he hadn't turned to marble.

What would it feel like to have those fangs sink into her flesh? Did rattlesnake bites kill? Hadn't she heard somewhere that very few people died from snakebites in the United States? Maybe she was about to become one of those statistics.

Stop it, she ordered herself. *Even if he strikes, he may not be able to reach this far. He may miss. Surely they miss once in a while.* Where would he hit if he did strike? He was on a level with her calves. Why hadn't she taken the time to put on her boots this morning? Surely the snake's fangs wouldn't be able to penetrate that wonderful, sturdy leather. If only she'd put on her boots. Wishing wouldn't make it so.

How long could she stand here? What if she passed out? Was a snake going to know the difference between an attack and a faint? She could feel beads of sweat breaking out between her shoulder blades. Despite the warmth of the sun, she was cold and clammy.

She couldn't stand here forever. She'd count to a hundred and then she had to move.

Where was Cody?

As if in answer to her thought, he was there. She felt a tremendous surge of relief. He'd know what to do. Her instinctive belief in his ability to help her had little to do with his obvious knowledge of the wild. Somewhere, deep inside, she knew she'd have had the same reaction if she'd been facing a mugger in downtown L.A. She believed in Cody Wolf in a way that had little to do with logic.

"Snake." Her mouth was so dry that the word came out with a sibilant hiss, which seemed vastly appropriate.

"I know. Don't move." He was somewhere off to the side. She couldn't make her eyes move enough to see him, but the quiet rasp of his voice told her his location.

"It's going to be okay. Just don't move."

Cody could feel sweat making his palms slippery on the barrel of the rifle. He'd told her it was going to be okay but how did he go about making good on that promise? The snake was coiled up in such a way that the only clean shot at him was from directly in front. And Sara and the dog blocked that angle. If he got too close, it could startle the big rattler.

For long moments the two humans, the dog and the snake were frozen in a tableau. Whether or not the snake knew it, he was proving just how helpless civilization could still be when face-to-face with nature.

Sara bit her lip to hold back a whimper. The tension spiraling upward threatened to break loose in a scream. Cody leaned the rifle against his leg and unbuttoned his heavy flannel shirt. If he couldn't get at an angle to shoot the rattler, maybe he could get close enough to throw the shirt over him. If he timed it just right, he could throw Sara out of the way before the serpent could wiggle free.

He jerked the shirt off his shoulders, slipping the rifle down to the ground. His fingers knotted around the shirt's hem. The weight of the collar would, he hoped, be enough to carry the blue-and-gold fabric over the snake. He took a step forward, feeling the ground beneath his moccasin before putting his weight on the foot. A snapped twig right now could mean the difference between success and disaster.

Sara trembled. She could sense that Cody was moving. What was he doing?

Just two more steps and he'd have to try. He wouldn't be able to get any better position than that. If Sara could just hold up a moment longer. He could almost smell her fear, almost feel the ragged rhythm of her pulse as if it beat in his own ears.

He eased one foot forward. His muscles knotted with tension. So close.

The rattler's head wove an uneasy pattern from woman to dog to man. It was impossible to judge what was going on behind those flat, reptilian eyes, impossible to guess what thoughts were going through the snake's mind. Whatever they were, he must have decided that he didn't like what he was seeing. After all, none of these three creatures was normal prey.

With a last irritated rattle of his tail, he uncoiled and slithered his way back into a crevice in the rock behind him. Dog growled low in his throat, throwing a final curse after the snake.

Sara couldn't move. She could only stare at the ledge where the snake had lain. He was gone. The thought was totally beyond her dazed mind. Just like that, he was gone. Such a simple solution. A faint disturbance in the dust on the ledge was all that marked his passing.

She turned her head dazedly as Cody's fingers closed around her upper arm.

"Sara?" His eyes had darkened to almost forest green, his features had softened with concern. He looked so solid, so secure. Sara blinked and then blinked again, trying to wash away the burning sensation in her eyes. She was surprised by the feel of tears on her cheeks. Was she crying?

Cody looked into the drowned amethyst of her eyes and his heart gave a painful thump. Without conscious thought, his fingers slid from her arm to the back of her head, pulling her forward.

"It's all right. You probably scared him as much as he scared you. Once he figured out that you weren't going to attack him and you weren't edible, he just got disgusted and left. You're all right now."

Sara was surprised to find her face pressed against his bare chest, his voice rumbling into her ear. She didn't quite remember how she came to be there, but she didn't move. His skin was warm and slightly damp. The mat of hair tickled her nose a bit but it was a good feeling. Her arms felt so natural resting around his waist.

She was so tired. Tired of being strong. It had been so long since she'd been able to lean on someone. When her brother died she'd become half-sister, half-mother to a growing boy, faced with earning a living and creating a home. It just felt so good to be able to rest on someone else—just for a moment.

The feelings her soft weight aroused in Cody were far from restful. For the first few seconds, all he was aware of was the tremendous relief of knowing she was all right. He held her close, absorbing her quiet tears as if they were his own. Gradually, he became aware of the pressure of her breasts on his chest, with only the thin layers of her clothes between them. The warm scent of her. The silk of her hair in his fingers.

His hands moved to cup the back of her head, tilting her face up. Perhaps he only intended to tell her that she was safe now. Maybe he only meant to brush the tears from her cheeks. His motives were too tangled for him to read.

Sara's eyes were closed, her lashes creating a spiky pattern on her flushed cheeks. Slowly they fluttered upward and her eyes met his. Cody's head dipped, his movements slow, uncertain. Sara let her eyes close again, holding her breath as his lips brushed over the dampness of her cheek. He seemed to sip the tears from her skin, taking away the chill of fear and leaving behind a gentle warmth that sank deep within her.

Her lips parted, her breathing became shallow as his mouth touched her face in light butterfly kisses. His hands tightened on the back of her head, tilting her face back as he tasted the delicate length of her jaw. There were no tears there but Sara didn't care. There was a tingling sensation low in her belly, a sensation that grew with each touch of his mouth.

When his lips at last settled on hers, she let go her breath in a long sigh. She didn't need his urging to come up on her toes, arching closer to him. His mouth was warm and hard, urging her lips to part, seeking access to the tender inside flesh of her mouth. His tongue rubbed lightly along the inner surface of her lower lip before slipping inside.

Sara's hands slid up his back, seeking something to cling to as his tongue engaged hers in a delicate duel. His hands eased out of the tangled silk of her hair and slid down her spine, his fingers exploring every curve, setting the nerve endings to life. He hesitated in the small of her back, his thumbs drawing circles there as the kiss deepened.

Her tongue came out to trace the hard line of his teeth, and as if it were a signal he'd been awaiting, Cody's hands slid over her buttocks, lifting her easily until her toes left the ground. His legs braced apart, he drew her into the cradle of his hips.

Sara moaned from deep within her throat, feeling the hard pressure of his arousal against the softness of her femininity; only a few tantalizing layers of cloth separated them. She buried her fingers in the shaggy blackness of his hair, arching her hips as if trying to transcend the physical barriers between them. Without the rough denim on his legs, he'd be silk and steel against her, within her. Her stomach clenched at the thought.

She'd never felt like this before. Never wanted anyone the way she wanted this man. Certainly not David. Dear, sweet David had never made her feel this primitive, this elemental. David! Oh, my God! What was she doing?

Cody felt her mental withdrawal long before he felt the physical pressure of her hands on his arms pushing him away. His arms tightened for a moment in denial and he felt her draw in a sharp breath of fear. With much effort, he released her, and Sara backed away shakily.

Around them the little valley was full of sunshine and the clean scents of nature. But neither of them noticed anything outside the circle of shimmering tension that held them in place. Sara's shaken retreat had carried her only a foot or two away. They were still so close that she could see the golden flecks that burned in the clear green of his eyes. Cody could see the enticing peaks of her nipples through the cloth of her shirt and, for just an instant, he wanted to ignore her protest and pull her down into the grass and make love to her.

He felt exhilarated, frustrated and aroused. Couldn't she see that this was inevitable? Why was she backing off? He was savagely excited, hungry. But looking at the uncertainty and fear in her eyes, he suddenly had an image of how he must look to her. His shirt lay on the ground behind him and the autumn sun shone on skin turned bronze by summer's sun. His jeans rode low on his hips, the Apache boots clung lovingly to his calves, the black haft of his knife rested snugly in its sheath. He hadn't had a haircut in weeks and his hair was shaggy, black and untamed.

He looked every inch the savage Indian, and he felt his stomach tighten at the shock he read in her eyes. He'd seen that look before in a woman's eyes: shock and a kind of sly excitement. There was something about the forbidden pleasure of letting a savage make love to them that excited some women.

He'd come to terms with that reaction a long time ago and had learned to either avoid women who felt that way or ignore it. But seeing that shock overlaying the awareness in Sara's eyes infuriated him. He wanted to bury his hands in her hair and crush those soft lips beneath his. He wanted to erase that look in her eyes.

"I'm sorry. I don't usually—"

"Let a savage touch your lily-white skin?" Cody's words cut into her sentence, and there was so much bitter anger in them that it took Sara a few minutes to make sense of what he was saying.

"Don't worry," Cody continued. "I've never been known to leave permanent stains. It's amazing what a little soap and water will do."

"That's not—"

"Horrified that you responded to me?" The mouth that had so recently driven every thought from her head curved in an ugly sneer. "A lot of women like the taste of forbidden pleasure. After all, I'm safe enough. Indians are tame these days. Of course, I'm only half Indian. A half-breed." He spit out the last word, his eyes glittering emerald sparks.

"Does that excite you even more? Too bad I'm not in the market for a quick tumble in the grass. Maybe some other—"

He'd bent to pick up his shirt, and as he straightened her palm caught him full across the cheek. Not with a ladylike tap, but with a roundhouse swing that had the full force of her arm behind it. Taken off balance, he staggered slightly and almost sat down hard on the ground. The sound of the slap echoed in the quiet valley. Dancer looked up from the particularly succulent patch of grass he'd been munching and studied the two humans for a moment before returning to his meal.

"What the hell?" Cody's fingers explored the tender flesh on his cheek.

Sara stood in front of him, not in the least intimidated by the angry green fire that built in his eyes. "You are without a doubt the most arrogant, obnox-

ious SOB it has ever been my misfortune to meet!''
Cody blinked at her vehemence, but she went on before he could interrupt. Her hands clenched into fists
by her sides, she stared up at him, completely unconcerned with the fact that he was physically capable of
breaking her in two if he so desired.

"How dare you accuse me of something like that? I
don't care if you're half Venusian. The only thing I care
about is your ability to find my nephew. I'm not excited by anything about you," she lied without hesitation. "I've met bill collectors whom I found more
appealing and a hell of a lot more intelligent. I'm not
in the habit of jumping into bed with men I barely
know," she said, thereby tacitly admitting that that was
the reason she'd drawn away from him.

"Now, if you're through insulting me, it seems to me
that we should be getting on our way, if you don't
mind."

She stalked back toward camp, leaving Cody staring
after her with the feeling that he'd just picked up a kit-
ten only to have it turn into a puma. He rubbed absently at his burning cheek and then slid his arms into
the sleeves of his shirt.

He became aware of Dog, sitting in the grass a few
feet away, his yellow eyes watching Cody with interest.

"Well, what are you looking at?" Dog blinked but
didn't bother to move. With a snarl that would have
been more appropriate coming from the dog, Cody
jerked his shirt closed and began randomly thrusting
buttons through buttonholes. His long legs ate up the
distance to the camp, where Sara kept her back to him
as she rolled her sleeping bag.

Not another word was spoken until Cody moved to saddle the horses. Though every muscle in her body still protested when she moved, Sara was more determined than ever to show him that she could carry her own weight. She reached for Satin's saddle, feeling her shoulders creak as she lifted it. How on earth was she going to get it clear up onto the mare's back?

Setting her chin stubbornly, she shuffled her way over to where Satin stood. The mare turned to look at her, and Sara thought she saw a look of pained resignation in those big brown eyes. She looked from the saddle to her goal and wondered if Satin had grown a foot taller since yesterday. With a muttered curse, she braced herself to swing the heavy leather saddle up onto the mare's back. Satin had turned her head away, as if she couldn't bear to watch the operation, and Sara murmured an apology.

She took a deep breath and started to lift ... only to almost lose her balance when the load was suddenly taken from her hands. Cody swung the saddle up easily, setting it on Satin's back as if it weighed no more than a basket woven of reeds. Sara turned, an angry protest ready to spill out. Her logic told her that she'd never have gotten the saddle high enough, but illogically she couldn't see that that gave him any right to interfere.

"You'd never have made it," he said flatly, not even bothering to look at her.

Sara's indignant protest died unborn as he turned and walked away. With a gesture that could only be labeled huffy, she spun back to the horse and finished saddling her. But her problems weren't over. Once the animal was saddled, there came the problem of getting her posterior into that saddle. There was no excuse for putting off the attempt. Cody had already cleared the camp and loaded the pack animals with his usual disgusting efficiency.

She didn't hear him approach, but the sudden warmth at the back of her neck warned her as clearly as if he'd been wearing bells on his toes. He stopped right next to her, but Sara pretended to be very absorbed in studying the smooth leather of the saddle. She wasn't ready to meet those eyes yet. A tiny voice of caution warned her that looking into those brilliant eyes could be dangerous.

"I'll give you a boost up." His husky voice sent a shiver up her spine. The feeling was, of course, revulsion.

She cleared her throat. "That's okay, I can—"

"No, you can't. I don't want to waste time arguing. Put your boot in my hands and I'll toss you into the saddle."

Sara eyed the offered hands suspiciously. They were cupped at knee level, and looked warm and strong and more than capable of tossing her right over the top of the horse. Hesitantly, she set her booted foot in them and then gave a startled gasp as the muscles in his arms bulged and she was suddenly sitting in the saddle with no clear memory of how she'd gotten there. She turned to thank him but he was already gone, striding toward his own horse.

She dragged her eyes away from that long-legged walk, trying not to remember the way his jeans molded the muscles of his thighs. Trying not to remember anything at all about him. She gathered the reins in her gloved hands and took a deep breath. She had to keep her thoughts focused firmly on getting to Cullen. There was danger in allowing herself to be sidetracked by emerald eyes and a mouth that promised a glimpse of heaven.

Besides, she had to remember David. Dear, sweet David, who'd been so good to her. David, who wanted her to marry him. Why was it so hard to remember just what he looked like?

Chapter Six

They rode upstream, walking the horses along the edge of the streambed. Cody was vividly aware of the woman who rode behind the pack animals. She wasn't far enough away. But then, maybe there was nowhere on earth where she would be far enough away. He had the uneasy feeling that he wasn't going to be free of her just because she was out of sight.

He muttered a curse. She was sinking into his very soul. Under other circumstances he could have walked away before it was too late. But there was nowhere to go. No way to escape the spell she wove so gracefully.

He drew Dancer to a halt, leaning down out of the saddle to pick up the wicker basket he'd abandoned earlier. The trout were gone, but he'd expected nothing else. Without careful examination, there was no way to know what kind of a creature had raided his catch. Coyote perhaps, maybe a fox. With a shrug, he tied the basket onto the saddle and clicked his tongue at Dancer, urging the stallion into a walk again. He was in no mood to stop for a trout breakfast, and he doubted if Sara was, either. Whatever had taken the fish was welcome to them.

Sara looked up as Satin halted and then held her breath. Cody was leaning so far out of the saddle, she was sure he was going to fall on his head at any moment. He picked something up off the ground and tied it onto his saddle. Without looking back, he started Dancer in motion again and the pack horses obediently trailed along after him, followed by Satin.

Sara relaxed her body into the saddle, ignoring her aching muscles. She was in good shape; it wouldn't take long for her to adjust to this mode of travel. Besides, even if she were crippled for life, all that really mattered was finding Cullen.

Cullen was all she cared about. He was all she had. He was her younger brother and best friend in one package. She'd valued his pragmatic outlook on life almost since he'd learned to talk. He'd inherited all of Evan's calm control and practicality, and in many ways she'd depended on Cullen as much as he had on her.

She was ashamed to admit that for a little while, wrapped in Cody's arms, she'd almost forgotten the reason they were here. His mouth had driven every thought from her except the elemental needs he aroused. She lifted her free hand and touched her mouth uncertainly. Even through the leather of her gloves, she could almost feel the heated legacy of that kiss.

Her eyes swept to his back. She didn't have to close her eyes to remember the feel of those corded muscles beneath her fingers. It was just the situation, she told herself, refusing to acknowledge the doubtful note in her own thoughts. She'd been frightened half out of her wits and he'd been there to offer her a strong shoulder to lean on. Even now she shuddered when she remembered those minutes spent staring at the rattle-snake, wondering when he'd choose to strike.

Propinquity. That was it. He'd been there when she was feeling weak and frightened. It had nothing to do with jewel-green eyes and long-fingered hands that teased along the muscles of her back as if she were made for his touch alone.

She sighed, realizing the direction her thoughts were taking. She was just going to have to watch out and make sure that things didn't get out of hand. Cody Wolf was dangerously tempting.

By the time they stopped for a simple lunch of cold beans and Spam, the hostility that had marked the be-ginning of the day's journey had faded away. Surrounded by the mountains, nature's magnificent handiwork, on all sides, it was impossible to hold on to petty hostilities. Something about the solidity of the land they traveled, the massive age of the peaks, made everything else seem unimportant.

They ate their cold meal in silence, but it was a comfortable silence. If Sara found herself avoiding his eyes, she refused to admit it. He'd dismounted and walked back to help her off her perch before she could force her sore muscles into action. He hadn't said anything as he put his hands around her waist and lifted her easily, as if her weight meant nothing to him. Her skin still tingled with the imprint of his impersonal help.

She'd been too angry this morning to concern herself with appearances, but when Cody glanced across the few feet that separated them, she was suddenly vividly aware that her hair was still tangled, her face unwashed, her shirt wrinkled from being slept in. She finished the last bite of her beans in a gulp before murmuring something incoherent and getting to her feet.

She could feel his eyes following her as she pulled a few necessities out of her saddlebag and walked downstream until she was out of sight behind a huge boulder. When she returned, she felt much more human. She'd brushed her hair and cleaned her face, applying a thick layer of moisturizer and sunscreen. The sun felt gentle on her face, but at this altitude she couldn't afford to take it for granted. Sunburned models were not in great demand. There wasn't much she could do about her shirt because all her clothing was packed on the packhorses. But she had dampened a cloth and taken a rough sponge bath with cold stream water, and that plus fresh underwear went a long way toward making her feel cleaner.

Cody lifted one brow in comment when she returned to the camp but he didn't say anything, and Sara couldn't decide whether that lifted brow was sardonic, approving or bored. His impassive features gave nothing away. He'd cleaned up their luncheon plates and she was guiltily aware that so far on this trip she hadn't exactly pulled her weight.

He cupped his hands without a word, and she let him lift her into the saddle in matching silence. Starting when they stopped for the night to make camp, she'd show him that she could be an asset, not just another package to be hauled up the mountain. She watched him mount Dancer and start their small cavalcade in motion. She refused to ask herself why Cody Wolf's opinion of her was important. And, most of all, she refused to remember those explosive moments in his arms.

IF SARA WASN'T EXACTLY an equal partner in setting up camp that night, she did what she could. She didn't have his skill with the horses or in setting up the tent, but she managed to prepare a reasonably appetizing dinner using the packages of dried food Cody provided.

They ate without speaking, both of them savoring the meal with appetites sharpened by the fresh air and a full day's riding. Night fell as they ate, easing the world outside their campfire into darkness. With Cody holding the flashlight, Sara washed their plates in the stream.

When they settled back down beside the fire, there was a pleasant feeling of companionship between them. If tensions still shimmered beneath the placid surface, they were both fairly successful at ignoring them. Cody got out the silver flask and held it up questioningly. After a moment's hesitation Sara nodded, and he poured some cognac into one of the tiny silver cups that formed the lid of the flask.

"Clever." She nodded to the flask as she accepted the drink from him, being careful that their fingers didn't touch. If Cody noticed her avoidance, he didn't comment.

"It was my great-grandfather's. He got it from a traveling tinker in Oklahoma. He traded buffalo hides for it."

Sara longed to ask questions about his heritage, but remembering his sensitivity this morning, she bit her lip, afraid of offending him. Cody's eyes swept across the fire to hers, seeing the curiosity there. His spine stiffened automatically, but he could read nothing beneath that interest except a genuine curiosity, just as he was curious about her. He hesitated, startled by the realization that he wasn't offended by her interest.

"He was Comanche." He brought the word out with pride, watching for her reaction.

Sara shook her head. "About the only thing I know about Native American peoples is prehistoric pottery. When you major in art, you don't get a whole lot else."

Cody sipped the cognac, letting the rich taste of it lie on his tongue for a moment before swallowing. He so rarely talked about his heritage, finding that it made many people uncomfortable. What was there about Sara Grant that made him want to talk to her?

"The Comanche were never a large tribe. They were horsemen through and through. All the plains tribes used horses, but the Comanche wove them into their lives, more than perhaps any other tribe. The horse was central to their culture and most contemporary accounts agree that there were no better horsemen. On horseback, they ruled their world."

"My family is typical American mongrel. It must be wonderful to know something about your ancestors."

Cody's mouth twisted. Wonderful. Yes, he was proud of his heritage, but he'd never have used the word "wonderful." He thought of his grandfather, clinging to the remnants of a culture that had all but died before he was born, and of his father desperately trying to deny his heritage. And his mother, trying to bridge the gap between her background and her husband's.

No, "wonderful" was not quite the term he would have used.

Sara leaned back against her saddle and stared into the fire, letting the husky words flow over her. She sensed that this was something he rarely spoke of, and it almost frightened her that he was willing to speak to her about it. It suggested ties she wasn't sure she was ready to face.

"Your eyes don't look Indian." She wasn't even aware of speaking until the words left her mouth, and she held her breath, afraid that she might have offended him. Looking across the fire, she was entranced by the gentle smile that curved his mouth.

"Sure, and don't you recognize the look of the Irish when you see it, lass?" His accent was respectable, but it was the glimpse of laughter that made it impossible to drag her eyes away.

"Irish?"

"My mother was a true daughter of the old country. Her grandparents immigrated at the turn of the century, and her mother married a man from Ireland. I got my eyes from her. She used to claim that she carried a shamrock with her until I was born and the green of it tinted my eyes."

Sara could hardly believe the transformation that came over him when he spoke of his mother. There was an almost-boyish softness to his mouth that made her want to run her fingers across his lips just to make sure it was real.

He seemed to suddenly realize how much he was revealing. His mouth firmed, not angrily, but as if making sure that the barriers were back in place. He swallowed the last of his cognac and replaced the little cup on the flask. Sara gave a sigh of regret but followed his example, letting the last sip of cognac warm her throat before handing him her cup. Their fingers brushed and her eyes swept to his, wondering if she had been the only one to feel that electrical charge. His gaze held hers for an instant, and she read in it an awareness that told her he felt the same pull.

He looked away and the spell was broken. Broken but not forgotten. He moved out of the firelight to check on the horses, and Sara's eyes followed him until the darkness swallowed his lean form. Then her gaze was drawn inevitably to the tent he'd erected while it was still light. Tonight, they would share that small space. Her fingers trembled slightly as she touched her mouth, remembering this morning.

When he kissed her the terror she'd experienced when faced with the rattlesnake had evaporated like morning dew confronted by a hot summer sun. An apt comparison, because heat was exactly what she'd felt in Cody's arms. She'd been burning up, and had never experienced anything like the need she'd felt in his arms.

With a broken sigh, she pulled her hand away from her mouth. It was just that the situation had been extraordinary. She'd been in fear for her life. It was natural for that emotional buildup to break loose when he kissed her. It was nothing really personal.

She shook her head, unable to convince even herself that that was all it was.

She jumped, startled, as Dog trotted into the firelight. With a laugh she relaxed, realizing how tense she'd become. Nothing was going to happen tonight. Nothing that she didn't choose to let happen, a sly little voice within her hinted. She wasn't going to choose to let anything happen, she told herself firmly. She and Cody would share the tent like two intelligent adults forced into an awkward situation.

She reached for her hand lotion and began to smooth a quantity of it into her slender fingers. The habit of taking care of her hands was a long-established necessity. She couldn't afford to neglect them now. When she and Cullen got back to L.A., she was going to need all the work she could get to pay David back. Hopefully, she could avoid selling the house.

Dog padded around the fire and flopped down on her feet, his heavy body all but smashing her toes. She'd taken off the boots she wore for riding and put on more-comfortable sneakers, and the canvas did little to protect her toes from his weight. She started to shove him off and then stopped. He wasn't really hurting her and there was a certain comfort to his presence.

She finished spreading the lotion over her hands and arms, letting the familiar motion soothe her. Right after Evan died, Cullen had sometimes helped her rub lotion into her arms. She smiled tenderly, remembering his intense young face. He'd been so worried that taking care of him would be too much for her, so determined to do everything he could to help her. And so frightened. They'd helped each other get through that time, had become the best of friends. It wasn't possible that it was all going to end so soon.

To Cody, stepping silently into the firelight, she was a madonna and a temptress in one slim form. Her expression was so tender that he knew she was thinking of her nephew, and yet the gentle motions of her hands seemed to beckon like a siren's song. He wanted to feel those fingers on his skin. He wanted to bury his hands in that golden fall of hair and feel her mouth soften beneath his.

Sara glanced up, and he shook off his thoughts. He was becoming too wrapped up in this woman. There was a danger in that. He didn't want any involvement with a woman whose life ran along a path so far removed from his own. He'd spent too many years watching his parents try to bridge that gap in their marriage.

The powdery scent of Sara's hand lotion was carried on the wood smoke, creating a not unpleasant combination. It made him think of how nice it would be to have a woman to come home to. Someone to share his triumphs and failures. Someone to lie beside him in bed at night.

He muttered a curse and began putting out the fire with movements that reflected his anger. Dog stood up and moved out of the light, apparently deciding not to risk Cody's temper. Sara got to her feet uncertainly, wondering what had happened to upset him.

"I want to get an early start in the morning. The sooner we get started, the sooner this damn trip will be over."

Sara bit her tongue on the questions that bubbled up. If he wanted to throw a tantrum, she wasn't going to encourage him by noticing it. Her tone was the very essence of polite acceptance.

"Sounds good to me. The sooner we find Cullen and Bill, the better."

Half an hour later, she was debating the possibilities of sleeping outside. Coyotes, mountain lions and bears seemed like a better risk than the tension that permeated the little tent. Cody had politely suggested that she could have the tent to herself while he finished securing the camp, and Sara had been grateful for the few moment's privacy. She used it to shimmy out of her jeans and quickly brush her hair before crawling into the thick protection of her sleeping bag. She'd actually been half dozing when he ducked in through the low entrance.

All possibilities of sleep disappeared the moment he entered the small enclosure. Immediately, the tent seemed to shrink to a size that couldn't possibly hold both of them. Sara listened to the quiet rustle of cloth and tried not to imagine what he was doing. Was he taking off his jeans as she had done? What if he was going to sleep in the nude? What if he was? she demanded irritably, trying to slow her suddenly accelerated breathing. It was dark. If he wanted to strip buck naked, it had nothing to do with her. But the brisk mental admonition didn't stop her imagination from presenting her with amazingly detailed pictures.

It was even worse when the rustling stopped and she knew he was in his sleeping bag. Less than a yard separated them. If he stretched out his arm, he would be able to touch her. Not that she wanted him to do that, of course.

She lay flat on her back, eyes wide open and staring at the dark fabric over her head. Every little sound, every imagined move, added to her awareness of the man who lay such a short distance away. This was ridiculous. She had to get some sleep. But how could she sleep with him so close? Why didn't he do something? Say something? Was she the only one to feel this tension?

Despite her thoughts, Sara jumped as if he'd shouted when he spoke from out of the darkness, even though his husky words were hardly above a murmur.

"You can relax. The days when ignorant savages automatically raped helpless white women are long gone. I only attack when the moon is full, so you should be safe for a few more days."

There was a wealth of weary bitterness in the words, and after a moment of shocked silence, Sara felt anger burn away her nervousness.

"That chip on your shoulder may give you some kind of satisfaction, but I'm sick of your throwing it in my face. I wouldn't know about your background if you weren't so damn paranoid about it. And the next time you accuse me of prejudice, I'll...I'll..." she searched briefly for an appropriate threat "...I'll scalp you."

Her breathless little speech left an echoing silence in the tent, and she suddenly realized that she could have mortally offended the only man who could help her get to Cullen. His quiet laugh shivered through her.

"I stand corrected. Pardon my paranoia. I'll try to control it in the future."

"Good." All the anger had drained out of her. She couldn't believe she'd actually scolded him like that.

"Get some sleep. It's going to be a long day tomorrow. Good night."

"Good night." Silence settled over the tent, but the small confrontation seemed to have cleared the air. Sara was still vividly aware of his presence, but she found that it wasn't that difficult to close her eyes. Once they were closed, it didn't take long for her to fall into a deep dreamless sleep.

Cody listened to her breathing even out and steady. His mouth curved in the darkness. The problem with throwing up barriers between himself and Sara Grant was that he was finding he actually liked the woman. He couldn't even convince himself that it was only sexual attraction that drew him to her. He liked her. She'd made him smile in the few days since she'd shown up on his ranch—more than he'd smiled in years.

He closed his eyes. It was all right to like her, but that was as far as he could let it go. He couldn't afford anything more.

He didn't know how long he'd been asleep when the dream began to weave itself into his mind and he let himself be drawn into its pattern. He floated above the mountains, seeing the path they were to take as if it were marked on a map. That was enough. It was all he needed. But the dream held him fast.

The scar of the plane's landing was gouged out of dirt and rock, cut into the land as if by a giant's knife. Angry and violent. The plane was a crumpled mass of silver and red. Silver pain and red blood. Incongruously, mountain columbines suddenly sprouted beside the wreckage, covering it with healing purple. The purple flowers shifted and changed, and he was looking into Sara's thick-lashed eyes, their expression demanding, pleading, holding out a promise he was afraid to reach for.

Sara roused sometime in the night. Outside, everything was still, but across the short space that separated them, Cody stirred restlessly. She raised her upper body on one elbow, squinting through the darkness. His body was only a darker shadow among shadows, but she could see movement as he twisted back and forth. He was muttering—that was what had awakened her.

"Silver. Twisted silver." The words were barely audible and she leaned closer, wondering if she should wake him. "Scars. Columbine eyes. Too late. Too late."

The words snapped off abruptly, and obeying some instinct, Sara quickly huddled back down in her sleeping bag, eyes closed, forcing her breathing to steady. A second later, Cody sat up, his breathing ragged in the confined space. She could feel his eyes going over her as clearly as if he'd touched her. A moment later she heard the rustle of clothing, and then he ducked out of the tent.

She opened her eyes and stared after him. What had he been dreaming about? It was a long time before he came back to bed, and Sara found that she couldn't go back to sleep until he returned. His presence was important in some way she couldn't quite define. Or perhaps she was afraid to try to define it, for fear of what she might find out about her feelings.

As HE'D PROMISED, they started out early the next morning. Though her muscles still protested sullenly when she mounted her horse, she wasn't as stiff as she had been. Her body was adjusting to the conditions. Even the thin air was beginning to seem normal to lungs more accustomed to sea level.

Satin didn't require any real guidance to follow the packhorses, and Sara let her mind wander. Mostly her thoughts were with Cullen. What was he doing and feeling? Was he badly hurt? Was he conscious? She refused to wonder if he was still alive. She clung to her belief that if he were dead, she'd be able to feel that. He and Bill were used to hunting and camping in primitive conditions. Bill had been a medic in the army. Between the two of them, they had more survival skills than any twenty people. They just had to be alive. And Cullen had to know she wouldn't give up until she found him.

All too often she found her thoughts drifting to the man who rode ahead of her. They'd barely spoken that morning in the bustle of breaking camp. But some of the tension had been eased by last night's confrontation.

What was he thinking of? she wondered. Was he as aware of her as she was of him, or did he forget her the moment she was out of sight? Perhaps that was one of the reasons he hadn't suggested that they ride side by side, though there was room for it. He probably liked being able to forget about her as long as they were traveling. The thought was depressing, but Sara refused to examine why it bothered her.

They stopped for lunch, and the cold meal was eaten in almost total silence. Stealing glances at him from under her lashes, Sara thought she detected traces of last night's disturbed sleep. The lines beside his mouth seemed deeper. He hadn't shaved since they left the ranch and the stubble on his chin gave him a scruffy look, which should have been unattractive but wasn't. He glanced up and Sara's eyes lowered. She could feel a blush coming up in her cheeks, and she cursed her pale complexion that blushed so easily.

"Dog doesn't like many people." The words were so far away from her own thoughts that it took Sara a moment to grasp them. Her eyes focused blankly on the hulking canine who'd once again planted himself firmly across her feet. Sensing her eyes on him, Dog turned his head, yellow eyes staring at her dispassionately.

She eyed Dog doubtfully. "I'm not sure he likes me."

Cody stood up, arching his back in a bone-popping stretch, and Sara tried not to notice the way the movement molded his jeans to the long muscles of his thighs.

He studied the big dog and the petite woman for a moment before bending down to scoop his hat off the ground and slap it on his head. "He likes you."

Sara's eyes traveled from the dog to the man and then scurried back to the dog again. Dog was safer to look at. He didn't give her that uncertain, breathless feeling that the man did.

"If you say so." She moved her feet tentatively, a little uneasy about disturbing the huge animal. With an almost human grunt, Dog surged to his feet and wandered off. Cody's eyes gleamed with amusement as he watched her.

"If Dog didn't like you, he'd stay away from you. He's not a cuddly animal, but he tends to stick close to people he deems worthy of his time."

Sara bent to pick up her own hat and looked at the animal in question for a moment longer before turning toward the horses. "I suppose it would be worse if he thought he was a lap dog."

She turned as she got to her horse, only to find that Cody was standing right behind her. As long as she lived, she didn't think she'd ever adjust to his silent walk. Her head tilted up to meet his eyes, reading the amusement there. His whole face softened when he was amused, losing the fascinating hardness that both attracted and frightened her.

"If Dog thought he was a lap dog, I'd have to scrape you up off the ground after he was done sitting on you."

She swallowed, trying not to notice the way his chest hair curled in the opening of his shirt. "Like I said, it could be worse." Could he hear the tremor in her voice?

He cupped his hands and she set her booted foot in them, letting him toss her into the saddle even though she'd managed to mount without his help earlier in the day. Once mounted, she looked down at him, a new perspective for someone who was accustomed to having everyone tower over her.

He reached up to scratch behind Satin's ear, his expression unreadable beneath the brim of his hat. Sara could only hope her own hat provided similar camouflage.

"Up ahead there's a place where the stream widens out into a pool. The water will be pretty cool but it might give you a chance to wash up, if you wanted. And it isn't as cold as it will be when the snow melts in the spring."

"It sounds wonderful. I must smell like a boar hog in June. But I don't want to slow us down."

"I'd planned to camp just a little ways downstream from the pool anyway. And I never knew a boar hog who smelled like a field of summer flowers."

He turned away to mount Dancer before Sara could respond. Had that been a compliment?

SHE STILL HADN'T DECIDED on the compliment when they made camp several hours later. It was still full daylight, though the sun was sinking fast. For the most part, she stood back and let Cody set up the tent and lay the fire. She wanted to pull her own weight, but there was no denying that she was more of a hindrance than a help when it came to setting up a wilderness camp.

"I'm going to ride on ahead and check out the trail. The pool is straight up the stream about fifty yards. Dog will stay with you."

Sara hesitated a moment, remembering the rattlesnake. She wasn't so sure she wanted to be left alone, though the thought of being able to wash up was like a promise of heavenly rewards.

"Don't worry about snakes. The one you met up with should have been tucked away for the winter already. You're not going to run into another one, especially not this close to nightfall. And Dog is enough to scare off anything else that might be around. I won't be gone long."

He'd stripped the saddle off Dancer when they first stopped and gave the stallion a handful of oats. Now he grasped a handful of silky mane and swung himself onto the horse's back. There was something so right about the way he looked sitting atop the gleaming bay without the artificial intrusion of the saddle to dull the contact between man and horse. His heels nudged the horse into motion, and with a sigh Sara turned to walk upstream, Dog trotting silently next to her.

"I hope you don't mind being elected to do guard duty. I really feel much better having someone around." There was something about Dog that made it seem perfectly normal to converse with him as if he were human. It didn't matter that he didn't have much to add to the conversation. Sara had the feeling that it was purely by choice that he didn't answer her remarks.

She found the pool without trouble, her breath catching at the sheer beauty of it. The stream widened and deepened long enough to form a peaceful little pool. Pine trees trudged down almost to the water's edge on the opposite bank. On the side where Sara and Dog stood, a blanket of grass—pale green with approaching winter—carpeted the shallow rise that banked the pool.

It was a perfect jewel of nature, and Sara just looked at it for a long moment, letting the peace of it seep into her bones.

Cody had told her that the water would be cold and he proved to be correct. But the chill wasn't enough to prevent her from stripping off her clothes and wading out into the water. It was only hip deep at its deepest, but the current made it necessary to take care with her balance. Holding her breath, she ducked her head under the water, surfacing with a shiver. She washed her hair briskly, giving a sigh of pleasure as several days of grime floated away. Pleasant though the water felt, it was too cold to linger in, and she hurried up onto the bank, rubbing her skin dry with a thin towel.

Once she was out of the water, the dying sun warmed her chill skin, and she didn't reach for her clothes immediately. It felt so wonderfully pagan to be standing naked in the fresh air. She stretched out her arms for a moment, arching her back and turning her face up to the light, letting her damp hair trail down her back as she luxuriated in the sheer pleasure of being alive.

Everything would work out just fine. Cullen was going to be safe and sound. When the world was this beautiful, it was impossible to believe otherwise.

The Survivor

CULLEN BLEW GENTLY on the infant flames, coaxing them to life. When they finally flickered up and caught on the fine twigs he'd layered over the bits of bark, he sat back slowly and dared to close his eyes for a moment. With his back to the granite wall behind him, he could afford to relax for just a moment.

Over his head, the granite arched forward to provide an overhang that served to shelter the little hollow he'd found. It was still broad daylight and he had the urge to keep moving, to make the most of the light hours. But the thought was sluggish and easily pushed aside.

His knee ached with a steady throbbing that felt as if it were tearing the joint apart. He'd bound it with a sturdy bandage, not knowing if it was the right thing to do but feeling that the damaged joint needed some support. He was so tired. Two days away from the crash and he felt as if it had been two weeks.

He forced his eyes open and edged himself into a sitting position. Forcing his cold fingers to move slowly and steadily, he added a few more pieces of twig to the small fire, finally daring to add a couple of good-sized sticks. With the fire burning steadily, throwing a bit of warmth into the little hollow, he turned his attention to a meal.

Lying limply on the rock beside him was a rabbit. He'd set a snare at yesterday's camp and this morning his effort had been rewarded, though he doubted if the rabbit had looked at it quite that way. He'd gutted the animal before starting on the trail, tying the carcass to his belt. He didn't want the entrails near where he was camping—they tended to draw predators. This way, he'd be long gone when nature sent in her cleanup crew.

It didn't take long to skin and butcher the small carcass, and soon the appetizing aroma of roasting meat filled the air. But despite the exercise, fresh air and the scent of the meat, Cullen had to force himself to eat. His appetite seemed to have been left back at the crash site along with everything else. He'd brought along only those things that he deemed essential to survival and everything else had been abandoned. A fitting memorial to Bill, he thought.

He had dried food, but there was no way of knowing how long it might have to last him. He had to supplement it as much as possible. He finished the last of the rabbit and forced himself to his feet, carrying the bones and hide as far from camp as he could manage and burying them.

He limped heavily back to the shelter of the overhang, sinking down on the rock, biting off a curse as his knee was jarred by the movement. His leg wasn't ever going to be normal again. The damage to the joint was too great and he was probably doing still more damage with every step he took. He considered the fact that he was probably going to walk with a limp for the rest of his life and then shut the thought away. There was nothing he could do about it. And, God knows, he was lucky to be alive at all.

He dragged the sleeping bag out and unrolled it, giving himself a bit of padding between the granite and his body. He'd gathered enough wood to keep the fire going all night. Looking out over the light snow that coated the ground, he wondered how long it would take him to walk to civilization.

It never occurred to him that he might not make it.

Chapter Seven

Cody's eyes were thoughtful as he guided Dancer back along the trail to camp. Their path had been smooth and easy so far, but it couldn't last that way much longer. The higher they climbed, the rougher the trails were going to get. The horses were up to it. He'd taken all of them into the high country before. All Sara would have to do was hold on to Satin and let the mare do the work.

Sara. Just her name brought a warmth to his chest. A feeling he didn't welcome at all. She was getting too close too fast. He didn't want the feelings she brought out in him. The sexual pull he understood and could deal with. It was an itch that could either be scratched by taking her to bed, or ignored, which he could handle. But this tenderness, this desire to protect her, this need to be close to her. Those were things new in his experience. New and unwelcome.

He shook his head as Dancer climbed up a small incline and they topped out on a rise. He had to stop thinking about her.

His thoughts scattered in a thousand different directions and his hands tightened automatically on the reins, drawing the stallion to a halt. Below him, he could see the stream they'd been following laid out like a shining bracelet amid the faded green of the grass. It was beautiful, but it wasn't what caused his heart to pound in slow, heavy thuds.

Beneath him, half-shadowed among the trees, was the shallow pool he'd told Sara about. If he'd thought about it, he would have assumed that she'd be back at the camp by now. Instead, she stood across the pool from where he sat on Dancer. The sun was almost down and the mountains threw long shadows across the narrow valley. But a few bright rays slipped around the hulking shoulder of the Rockies to spill onto the pool. The water glimmered gold, silver streaks marking the path of the current.

And Sara's body shone gold.

Cody thought he might suffocate on the rising desire that caught in his throat. The light gilded her body like a gossamer gown of palest amber. It caught on her hair, turning it to silver. As she turned, he could see the proud thrust of her breasts, the flat plane of her stomach and the shadowy triangle at the top of her thighs.

He couldn't move, couldn't think. All he knew was that he wanted her like he'd never wanted anything else in his life. It took every ounce of self-control he had to keep from slamming his heels into Dancer's sides and riding down off the hill to sweep her across his legs and carry her away to make love to her.

He closed his eyes, his hands shaking with need. There must be more of the untamed savage in him than he'd thought. Suddenly, he understood the appeal his ancestors had found in kidnapping a bride from another tribe. His mouth twisted ruefully as he opened his eyes. Take him away from civilization and all the savage came out in him.

Sara had slipped on her underwear while he struggled with his impulses, and he found himself resenting the thin bands of fabric that hid her from him. She tilted her head, and for a moment he thought she looked right at him, but then she turned away to pick up her jeans. If she'd known he was watching her, she would surely have shown some reaction. Probably furious indignation, he told himself. And he couldn't blame her. He had no right to be spying on her like this. It was an invasion of her privacy.

With an effort, he forced himself to nudge Dancer forward, and within seconds, the trees blocked the pool from sight. The stallion set a brisk pace through the trees, anxious to get back to camp and the oats that awaited him there.

They splashed across the stream above the pool and then turned to walk alongside the water. Somehow, Cody wasn't surprised to find Sara still standing next to the pool when he got there. She had just finished tying the laces of her sneakers and she got to her feet as he came into sight. Her hair fell down her back in a shining wave, her skin was flushed and clean, and he thought he'd never seen anything more beautiful in his life.

He drew Dancer to a halt and they stared at each other for a moment. It was impossible to read the expression in her eyes, impossible to guess at what she was thinking. Dog ambled over to sniff at Cody's foot and then, assured that he was relieved of guard duty, trotted off into the gathering dusk.

Without speaking, without taking his eyes off Sara, Cody rode the stallion forward. She watched them approach, and he thought he detected a shaken rhythm to her breathing. She didn't move even when the big horse stepped within inches of her feet. Her head was tilted back and there was a quality of challenge in her gaze.

Silently, he held out his hand, presenting his foot for her to use as a stirrup. Sara hesitated a long, silent moment and then bent to scoop her bundled clothing up off the ground. She set her free hand in his and he felt the electric shock of the contact all the way up his arm. Her foot came down on his and he pulled her up behind him, feeling her settle onto Dancer's back.

He dug his heel into the stallion's side and Dancer obediently started forward. The rocking motion of the horse's gait slid Sara forward until she was pressed to his back, and Cody sucked in a breath as her arm slid around his waist, holding him for balance. Her breasts against his back seemed to burn through the fabric of their clothing.

Sara wondered if he could feel the way her nipples hardened with his nearness. Leaning so close against his back, she could smell the faint salty tang of sweat brought out by a hard day's work. The scent was all male and amazingly provocative.

She wanted him.

The thought slipped into her mind not with the impact of a sudden discovery but with the quiet inevitability of something she'd known all along. She tried to shake the thought away. It was too soon. They were too different. She had never been inclined to jump into bed with a man unless she was thinking of a long-term relationship. There was no possibility of that here. Their lives lay along vastly different paths. They converged briefly at this point in time, but once Cullen was found her life would be in California, and Cody's life was here.

But she wanted him.

The short ride back to camp was silent. Cody pulled Dancer to a halt and slid off the stallion's back before reaching up to help Sara down. Her eyes avoided his, as if afraid of what she might read in them. He picketed the horse and then moved over to crouch in front of the tent. Sara tried not to notice the way his jeans molded to his thighs, the ripple of muscle as he leaned forward to breathe life into the fire.

Within minutes the fire was crackling cheerfully, and Cody stood up. She could feel him looking at her, but she kept her head bent over her pack, busily rearranging the contents as if it were vitally important.

"I'm going to wash up."

"The water's very nice." *Brilliant, Sara. Really a stunning bit of conversation.* She could feel his eyes on her but she didn't look up. What if he could read in her eyes how much she wanted him? There was a part of her that wanted him to cross the few feet that separated them and lift her to her feet, pulling her into his arms.

"Dog is around somewhere, and I'll just be at the pond. If there's any problem, just give a yell."

She nodded without looking up, and a second later he was gone. Her fingers, which had been so busily delving through the pack, suddenly went still and she slumped back against her saddle. Her hand was shaking as she shut the saddlebag and set it aside. The contents were a hopeless jumble, but she didn't care.

What was she going to do about Cody Wolf?

It would be insanity to get involved with him. They had nothing in common. Not like David. She had a lot in common with David. David lived in L.A. He understood her career. David loved her, wanted to marry her. She'd even been considering the idea. David was a nice man. She was fond of him. When he made love to her, it was a pleasant experience. It would be smart to marry David.

So why couldn't she remember what David looked like?

She almost moaned aloud with frustration. Why was it that, even now, all she could think about was Cody standing naked in the pond? The cool water glistening on his flesh, his legs braced slightly apart to stand against the current.

She shook her head, trying to shake away the vivid image. It was just the circumstances. She was dependent on him, not only for her own safety, but also for Cullen's rescue. He was the only hope she had. It was hardly surprising that some of her gratitude and the isolated situation should translate into a kind of sexual attraction.

Sexual attraction? That seemed to be a rather mealymouthed description of the way she all but burst into flames whenever he came near. And it had started the moment she first saw him, when she'd turned to find him at the bottom of the porch steps, and her heart had slammed against her ribs in a way that had nothing to do with being startled.

With a muttered curse, she surged to her feet and began preparation for the evening meal. Beyond the circle of firelight, darkness was complete. At another time, Sara might have been nervous about being alone among so much wilderness, but right now her own thoughts were more frightening than anything that could lurk in the dark.

Dog trotted into the firelight and sat down next to her, watching as she angrily stirred the freeze-dried packets of food into a meal. She set the pan next to the fire and sat back on her heels, reaching over to absently scratch the huge dog behind his ear.

Until then she hadn't voluntarily touched him, preferring to let him make any overtures that seemed appropriate. But the results of her automatic gesture were amazing enough to snap her out of her preoccupation. Dog's whole body stiffened and he let out a soft whimper before collapsing at her feet. Sara jerked her hand away, wondering if she'd triggered some primitive instinct that was going to result in his going for her throat.

But, looking down at him, she realized that his expression was one of absolute ecstasy. Hesitantly at first, she reached out to scratch his ear again, and his huge frame quivered with pleasure. The sight of the ferocious-looking animal reduced to a puddle of mush was enough to make her forget her disturbing thoughts. In fact, she welcomed the distraction. She was getting nowhere by going around and around in circles over her feelings for Cody.

When Cody stepped into the firelight, she looked up at him, her face alight with amusement. He stopped, caught by the glowing beauty of her, fighting the urge to draw her into his arms and crush the smile from her mouth.

"You could have told me it was all a put-on."

Her complaint held an undercurrent of amusement, and his eyes lowered reluctantly from her face to Dog, who lay at her feet, obviously a slave for life. There was such a look of bliss in Dog's narrowed eyes that Cody's mouth widened in a smile that matched Sara's.

"I see you found his weak spot." He bent to tuck his dirty clothes into a pack and then crouched down next to the fire.

"You might have told me that his ferocious exterior concealed the heart of Jell-O."

Cody's smile widened as he poured a cup of coffee from a battered tin pot. "Don't be fooled. If he thinks there is a need, Dog is more than capable of living up to his exterior." Dog lifted his head from where it had been resting against Sara's feet and blinked at Cody, his shaggy tail shifting in a shallow wag.

Cody reached out to scratch the dog's ear at the same moment that Sara moved to do the same thing, and their fingers touched. The light atmosphere popped as if it were a bubble that had drifted too close to a flame. The electric shock that surged through them at that contact was powerful enough to silence them both.

She pulled her hand back as if burned, which was just how she felt—burned by the heat that sizzled between them. She cleared her throat, willing her voice to steadiness.

"Supper's done."

They ate in total silence, and Sara had to force down every bite. She couldn't concentrate on anything except the man across the fire. No matter where her thoughts drifted, they seemed to come back to him. She wanted him to go away and take this disturbing new awareness with him.

She wanted him to cross the few feet that separated them and take her in his arms.

She wanted to scream with frustration.

They didn't sit by the fire talking that night. Something had happened during those moments by the pool and the short ride back to camp. It wasn't possible anymore to pretend to a casual friendliness. Whatever was between them could never be casual.

Sara crawled into the tent as soon as the evening meal was over and everything had been put away. Not that she could go to sleep, but she preferred to lie in her sleeping bag and stare at nothing rather than to sit out by the fire until the tension grew unbearable.

Somehow, in those moments by the pool, they'd lost the ability to keep things light. She stirred restlessly. Did he know that she'd seen him watching her? She flushed at the memory of that moment when she'd seen him above her. It was only a quick glimpse, but the image was indelibly etched in her mind.

With the sun behind them, he and Dancer had been little more than a bronze silhouette on the hill above the pool. She'd felt his eyes before she'd seen him. And she'd known he was watching her. The thought should have upset her. At the very least, it should have sent her diving for her clothing. She blushed in the darkness, remembering the way her breasts had seemed to swell. She'd enjoyed knowing his eyes were on her. She'd wanted it to be more than just his eyes.

She turned onto her side, drawing up her knees within the confines of the sleeping bag. Since Evan's death, she'd been totally in control of her own life. She'd had to be. With a young boy to care for, she couldn't afford to be anything else.

She hadn't eased that control, even for David. In the five years they'd known each other, he'd learned to deal with the fact that she wouldn't lean on him. A year ago, when their relationship eased from their being friends into their becoming lovers, that hadn't changed. But there was something about Cody Wolf that made her feel as if she'd lost control. As if their relationship was headed for some predetermined ending about which she had very little say.

Cullen. She had to concentrate on Cullen. He was the only really important thing right now. His rescue was all she should be thinking about. She closed her eyes, building a picture of her nephew in her mind. Shaggy blond hair and a thick blond mustache formed the frame for eyes as blue as a summer sky. At eighteen, he could easily pass for twenty-five. There was a maturity about him that made it easy to forget how young he really was.

Tears stung her eyes. He just had to be all right. Cullen had been the glue that held her life together, the driving reason behind everything she'd done since her brother's death. He'd been her little brother, her son and her best friend. She simply couldn't lose him.

She drifted to sleep with Cullen's image firmly in mind, only vaguely aware of the hard planes and angles of another face, intruding with emerald eyes, looking at her with a challenge she was not yet ready to answer.

She didn't stir when Cody slipped into the tent and crawled into his sleeping bag, but she woke in the night, again to his mumbled words and restless stirring. She stared through the darkness, listening to his staccato muttering. "Twisted silver and columbine eyes and death. Too late. Too late." Tonight, his nightmare didn't wake him, and at last he lay still and silent once more. Sara lay awake a little while longer, a fantastic idea forming in her mind.

THEY STARTED early the next morning after a cold breakfast of granola and reconstituted powdered milk. If Sara had hoped that last night's tension would disappear in the clear light of morning, she was doomed to disappointment. If anything, it seemed to have increased. Cody's restless sleep showed in the dark shadows beneath his eyes. Maybe that was why a shimmering tension seemed to surround him. She wasn't the only one to sense it. She noticed that Dog showed a distinct tendency to avoid him, and even Dancer seemed to shy away when Cody went to saddle him.

When all signs of their camp had been obliterated, Sara mounted Satin and waited while Cody ran a final check on the pack animals. When he mounted Dancer and started the stallion out, she abandoned her accustomed place behind the pack horses and nudged Satin up to walk next to Dancer. Cody threw her an unreadable glance from beneath the brim of his hat, and Sara gave him a wide, guileless smile, calling up every bit of acting ability she'd ever had to use in her modeling.

"It looks like a beautiful day."

He tilted his head to look at the clouds building along the tops of the mountains and then arched one brow in her direction. "We'll have rain before nightfall."

He fixed his gaze firmly ahead of them but Sara ignored the hint. There were things she wanted to know. "You must have spent a lot of time in the mountains."

"Quite a bit."

"You seem to know them so well."

"I don't claim to be an expert."

"Have you lived around here very long?"

"Most of my life."

Her hands tightened on the reins and Satin sidled a bit in protest. How was she supposed to find out anything when he answered practically in monosyllables?

"Do you do a lot of camping?"

"Not too much."

"Have you—"

"Look. Why don't you just come out and ask whatever it is you're angling for? And then I can tell you that it's none of your damn business."

The abrupt flash of temper cut through her words, startling her into silence. He hadn't even bothered to turn his head to look at her. The realization brought a matching flare of temper from her. She'd tried to lead up to it tactfully, but if he didn't want that, she'd just jump right in.

"How do you know where the crash site is?" She'd asked him once before, at the ranch, and he'd ignored the question. At the time, she hadn't really noticed the deliberate omission. It hadn't been important. But now she wanted an answer.

Cody's shoulders tightened as if she'd laid a whip across them, and Dancer reared in answer to some pressure from Cody's long fingers. Satin neighed nervously and twisted away from the bigger horse, and for a moment, Sara had her hands full controlling the mare.

When the two animals were again pacing quietly, Sara looked at Cody expectantly. When he didn't speak or look at her, she nudged Satin a little closer, frustrated by her inability to read his face. "Cody?"

"What?" The one word held a wealth of warning, but she refused to be intimidated.

"How do you know where to find the crash?"

"What difference does it make?"

"I don't think it's unreasonable to want to know that."

"Well, I do." The shock of his flat refusal to answer tightened her fingers on the reins, and in obedience to the signal, Satin stopped. Sara sat in silence for a long moment, watching Cody's back. When the second packhorse pulled level with her, turning to give her an indifferent look out of soft brown eyes, Sara pressed her heels against the mare's flanks and urged her forward until they were side by side with Cody and Dancer.

"I think—"

"Drop it."

"I won't drop it. I don't see—"

"Drop it, Sara!" And the look he gave her was so full of command that she found herself automatically obeying. Her hands tugged on the reins, and Satin gradually dropped back until they fell in line behind the second pack animal.

The day did not improve as it aged. The animals acted as tense and nervous as Sara felt. As the sun rose higher in the sky, it was gradually blocked out by the heavy bank of clouds that was building among the higher peaks. Whether it was the impending storm in nature or the suppressed storm between the two humans that was causing the problem, the horses were skittish and hard to control.

Sara found herself having to draw on her rather thin riding skills to keep Satin calm. The mare showed a tendency to shy away from anything that moved, and as the wind picked up, there were more and more things that moved. Bushes, trees, the wind itself—all seemed to offer some threat that Satin was determined to avoid. It was like being on a carnival ride, never knowing when the horse was going to spook one way or another. Sara let her body relax in the saddle, swaying with the mare's movements, keeping her hands firm on the reins.

When lunchtime rolled around, Cody halted just long enough to hand her a chunk of beef jerky.

"There's a cave about two hours' ride from here." His eyes scanned the horizon and Sara could hear the concern in his voice. "I think we've got time to make it before the storm hits. Are you managing okay?"

His eyes settled fully on her and she felt the impact clear to her booted toes. The brim of his hat shadowed his face, making it all angles and planes, his eyes unreadable dark pools. She reached up to tug her own hat farther down over her eyes, as if it could offer her some protection.

"I'll be all right."

He nodded. "Once the storm actually breaks, the horses will calm down." He leaned forward to lay his hand against Satin's neck, crooning softly to her. The mare calmed instantly, as if she'd never known a nervous moment in her life. "It's the waiting that upsets them. Just talk to her and keep a strong hand on the reins and you should be okay."

He turned Dancer and rode back to the pack animals. Sara watched him, feeling as if he'd laid a soothing hand on her also. She chewed on her jerky, taking some of her uncertainty out on the chewy piece of meat. The animals weren't the only ones who didn't like storms.

By the time they reached the cave, it was hard to say who was more tense, Sara or her horse. The ride had been exhausting. As the clouds grew darker and heavier and the wind picked up, Satin had danced skittishly at every blowing leaf. It was as if she knew that nature was building up to something big and she didn't like the idea of being out in it.

The opening of the cave was wide and inviting but Cody brought them all to a halt outside and swung down off Dancer. Sara held out her hand automatically when he handed her Dancer's reins and the leading ropes of the two pack animals.

"I'm going to make sure it's still unoccupied." She shuddered and bit her lip on a protest when he drew his rifle out of the boot on Dancer's saddle.

Dog seemed to know that they'd arrived at a place where they were going to stay for a while. He'd ranged ahead of them all day, only returning once or twice as if to make sure that they were still following. Sara had the feeling that he could sense the tension between the two humans and preferred to avoid it. He slipped out of the forest and nosed Cody's hand, announcing his arrival. Cody bent to murmur a few words to him, and Dog's nose dropped to the ground outside the cave, sniffing the rocky floor as the two of them entered.

The minutes seemed to crawl by after they disappeared. The sky had darkened to a leaden gray that had the look of twilight more than midafternoon. Gusts of wind whipped the pine branches around, startling the horses into skittish prancing. Rain began to fall, just a light mist that did little more than moisten the landscape. But she didn't doubt that there was much more in store for them.

Dancer rolled his eyes, obviously not liking the situation at all, and Sara held her breath, praying that Cody would return before the storm broke in earnest. As it turned out, Cody and the storm arrived at the same moment.

He stepped out of the cave just as a flash of lightning lit the sky with eye-searing brilliance. Thunder followed on its heels. Sara saw Cody's mouth moving, but whatever he was saying was drowned out in the thunder's rumble. The reaction from the horses was instantaneous. Satin skittered in one direction, the packhorses in two others and Dancer went straight up.

Sara tightened her knees around Satin's barrel, trying to keep her balance. She managed to hold on to the mare's reins and one lead rope with one hand, but as he reared up, Dancer jerked loose his reins and the other lead rope. Beneath the dying roar of the thunder, Sara heard a shrill whistle and then a streak of black and white went by, following the path of the loose packhorse.

Dancer spun in a tight circle and then stretched his big body out in the start of a dead run, heading back the way they'd come. From the corner of her eye, Sara saw Cody run directly into the path of the frightened horse. Her hands knotted on the reins, drawing Satin to a startled halt. Though only seconds could have passed, Sara felt as if she aged a hundred years as she waited to see the stallion run right over the man.

Confused, Dancer slowed and swerved, trying to go around Cody. This was apparently just what Cody had been waiting for. In a movement almost too quick to see, Cody jumped forward, grabbing Dancer's mane and swinging himself into the saddle even as the stallion lunged into a full run.

Sara forgot how to breathe as she watched horse and man disappear at a dead run. The rain turned from a light mist to a steady downpour, dripping off the brim of her hat.

Moving automatically, she slid off Satin's back, feeling her knees tremble as her feet hit the ground. She leaned against the saddle for a moment, steadying herself. Now that the storm had actually arrived, the horses had calmed, and Satin allowed herself to be led into the cave without so much as a whicker of question. The packhorse followed the mare's lead, and within seconds they were all sheltered from the elements by the solid bulk of the mountain.

Sara unsaddled Satin and wrestled the packs off the other horse. She refused to think of what might be happening outside. She refused to even look outside. She felt as if all her emotions were frozen. She didn't even register surprise when Dog trotted into the cave, the other packhorse following behind, led by the reins gripped in the dog's teeth. She patted Dog absently and unloaded the pack, stacking it neatly in one corner.

He'd be back any second now. That was what she told herself as she rubbed the horses down. Any minute he'd walk through the entrance, leading Dancer. She kept repeating that as she forced her shaking hands to make a fire with the wood Cody had been gathering all day and tying to one of the packs. He'd be cold and wet and he'd probably welcome the fire. She scraped up handfuls of pine needles that had sifted into the cave over the years and used them as kindling, feeding the fledgling flames with bits and pieces of twigs until the fire was large enough to add the larger chunks of wood.

Any minute now, he'd come walking in. She gave each of the horses a ration of oats and fed Dog a double handful of dry food. She huddled next to the small fire, trying not to hear the pounding rain outside. Dog settled next to her and she welcomed his company, despite the pungent odor that filled the air as the fire began to dry out his coat.

What if Dancer had thrown him off? What if the stallion had tripped in a hole and broken his leg, or maybe he'd tripped and broken his leg and thrown

Cody over his head, and Cody was now lying out there in the rain, unconscious?

She put a brake on her feverish imaginings. Cody was a superb rider. He would be okay. Dancer had been too upset to be controlled without a battle. It would take some time.

Outside, the rain had turned to sleet, and it might as well have been night for all the sunlight that managed to penetrate the thick clouds. Higher up, it would be snowing. But she refused to even consider that. She could go crazy if she started thinking about Cullen and Cody both out in this weather.

She drew her knees up to her chest and tried to think of absolutely nothing. She didn't want to remember her parents, each dying while rain streamed down outside. Nor that Evan's plane had crashed in a storm. She didn't want to think of anything at all. She just wanted to hang on to her control.

When she heard a noise that managed to penetrate through the rush of the storm, she hardly dared to hope. Cody had set the rifle down just inside the cave and she'd brought it in farther when she was arranging their camp, and now her fingers closed over the stock and drew the rifle a little closer. The way her luck had been going lately, it was probably a bear looking for a place to hibernate for the winter.

Cody entered first. His flannel shirt was plastered to his body; his jeans were similarly soaked. The suede Apache boots had gone from light tan to dark brown and squished with every step he took. Water dripped from the brim of his hat. Behind him, Dancer paced tiredly.

Sara uncoiled slowly, torn by conflicting urges. She wanted to run forward and throw her arms around

him. She wanted to hit him for all the worry she'd gone
through. And she wanted to remain perfectly calm so
that he wouldn't know just how much she cared.

His eyes skimmed over the camp she had made—the
crackling fire, the sleeping bags neatly laid out not too
far from the heat, the horses dozing in the back of the
big cavern—and he nodded.

"You've put in a lot of work."

He led Dancer to the back of the cave and lifted the
saddle from the horse's back. Sara stood up as Cody
began to rub the stallion down, wiping the moisture
from his coat.

You've put in a lot of work. Was that all he had to
say? No explanation? No apologies? No concern for
whether or not she had been worried?

"You were gone a long time." Her voice was husk-
ier than usual, and if he'd been listening, Cody might
have heard the note of strain in it. But he was absorbed in feeding Dancer some oats and making sure
that the horse was dry enough. Satisfied that the stallion was all right, he turned and moved closer to the
fire, stripping off his wet shirt as he moved.

"I let him run some of the energy out." He tossed his
hat onto one of the packs as he spoke and ran his fingers through his hair, which was damp despite the hat's
protection. His torso glistened in the firelight as he bent
to dig through his pack for a fresh shirt.

Energy crackled around him as he thrust his arms
into the shirt's sleeves, and Sara's anger built as she
realized that he was actually enjoying the storm, just as
he'd undoubtedly enjoyed pitting his wit and strength
against the stallion's.

Cody turned to look at her, wondering at her silence. But whatever he'd planned to say was lost in the sharp crack of her hand connecting with his lean cheek. His head jerked to the side with the force of the blow.

"What the hell?"

Chapter Eight

"I've been sitting here worrying myself sick about you and you've been out playing some kind of macho game with that damn horse!" Sara could hardly see him through the blur of tears. Something had broken loose inside.

She'd been so frightened, so alone. Sure that something had happened to him. Convinced that she was going to lose both him and Cullen to yet another storm. Seeing him safe and sound seemed to have shattered all the control that had enabled her to get through her brother's death, raising a young boy on her own and then dealing with Cullen's disappearance.

Her hand was shaking as she lifted it again, but this time Cody caught it before her palm could connect.

"Sara, calm down."

"I don't want to calm down! I hate you. Do you hear me? I thought you'd been thrown off that stupid animal and you were lying out there somewhere bleeding to death in the rain." Her free hand formed a fist but his fingers wrapped around it before it struck his chest. Her shoulders were shaking with suppressed sobs as he pulled her to him. She resisted, but it was a weak resistance at best.

"I'm sorry. I didn't know you'd worry."

"I hate you." The words were muffled against his chest. He released her hands and his arms slid around her back, pulling her against the broad strength of his chest, offering her a place to rest her head.

Her fingers wound around the open edges of his shirt. Her nose was tickled by the curling hair that matted across his muscles. He smelled of sweat and rain and the outdoors. He felt so strong, as if he could easily brace her weight forever.

Cody bent his head over hers, his hands running soothingly up and down her back. She was such a slight weight against him. So fragile. It was hard to believe that such a slender body could hold such strength. The wild ride through the rain, the electricity that had been crackling between them for days, the isolation and her sweet warmth combined into a powerful force that drowned out all the cautions in his rational mind.

As if from outside himself, he saw his hand slide upward to bury itself in the hair at the nape of her neck. Sara's head tilted easily at his command, and he looked down into eyes the color of amethyst. His other hand slid down her back to press her closer, letting her feel the pressure of his arousal against her stomach. Her eyes widened and then fluttered shut as his head dipped and he kissed the traces of dampness from her cheeks.

The storm raged outside, pounding relentlessly against the ancient mountains, sending every creature that could move scuttling for shelter. Miles away, a mountain lion snarled its dislike of damp fur and slunk deeper into its lair.

Beside Cody and Sara, the fire flickered as a gust of wind blew into the cavern. But the rest of the world had faded to a far-away dream. Cody's fingers tilted Sara's head, giving his mouth access to the delicate line of her chin. His tongue teased every trace of tears from her skin, leaving a building warmth behind. Her mouth softened in anticipation of his touch, but he drew back. Her lashes lifted slowly, her eyes meeting the hot green of his. Beneath the hunger, she read a question. If she wanted, now was the time to draw back. Now was the time to say no. With a sigh, she tightened her hold on his shirt, pulling him closer, giving him the answer he needed.

His mouth sought hers, hesitantly at first, and then with growing hunger. And Sara responded with an equal hunger. Something in this man had been calling to her since the first moment they met. The one kiss they'd shared had only served to whet her appetite. Her hands inched their way around his neck, burrowing into the shaggy thickness of his hair, drawing him closer as she stood on tiptoe. Her slim body arched, her hips fitting into his thighs as if made to rest there.

Her mouth opened to his, inviting him to take possession. He tasted the heat of her response. Sara twisted her head to give him greater access to her mouth, her tongue coming up to fence with his.

Cody's hands left her back, easing her away. Sara murmured a protest but then sighed with satisfaction as his hands slipped between them. She waited for him to search out the buttons on her shirt, but he seemed in no hurry. His hands circled her rib cage, his thumbs resting on the lower swell of her breasts. She forgot how to breathe, waiting for his hands to move. It seemed like eons before his palms slid up to cup the weight of her.

Her breath left her in a shuddering sigh. Cody dragged his mouth from hers, trailing kisses down the length of her throat. His fingers shook as he struggled with buttons that seemed reluctant to yield. The front clasp of her lacy bra was dealt with more easily, but he hesitated a long moment before easing the fragile material aside.

He wanted her so badly. The thought slid into his mind, frightening him with the intensity of his need. It wasn't safe to want something this much. It opened the way for pain. But he had to have her.

Sara knew nothing of his tortured thoughts. All she knew was that she had finally stopped fighting her need, had finally given in to the irresistible pull of desire. Something that felt this right couldn't possibly be wrong. And, right or wrong, she wasn't strong enough to fight it.

She moved a step away and Cody's hands tightened on her rib cage. No matter what his doubts, he didn't want to let her go, didn't think he could bear to let her go now. A twist of her shoulders eased the shirt away, and it fell to the hard ground of the cave. The firelight cast dancing shadows over her body. She stood before him, stripped of civilization's protective layers. She offered herself to him in the most elemental way possible. Need slammed through him. She was so perfect. Almost too perfect to touch. His hands slid upward, and Sara thought she would surely die from the sheer completion she felt as his hard palms at last cupped her breasts. She'd waited days, months, all her life for him to touch her like this.

Cody worshiped the beauty of her with his eyes for a long silent moment before he leaned forward and his lips closed around one pink nipple. His beard rasped against her soft skin. And suddenly all their slow passion disappeared in a surge of heat. Where a moment ago they'd had all the time in the world, now they had to have each other immediately.

He fought the fastening of her jeans while she struggled to pull the loose shirt from his shoulders. Somehow, they were at last freed of their clothing. His jeans hit the stoney ground and were kicked aside, and Sara's breath caught in her throat at the pure male beauty of him. Firelight flickered over lean muscle and coppery brown skin. The mat of hair on his chest tapered across his stomach in beckoning swirls before widening across his thighs, a path her fingers itched to explore.

Cody stood frozen, unable to read her stillness. Was she going to turn him away now? His lungs ached with the need for air as her fingers came out to lightly trace the dark curls that covered his chest. He couldn't drag his eyes from her face, the almost childlike curiosity in her expression. But there was nothing childlike about the way her small fingers closed around him. His breath left him in a groan, and her eyes lifted to meet his.

"You're beautiful, like a painting of a pagan warrior," she whispered.

His smile was shaky, and it was a struggle to make his hands gentle when he reached for her. Need boiled in him, urging him to slake his hunger now.

"You're the one who's beautiful. Fragile yet strong. Your hair is like morning's first light—shining promise." His fingers sifted through the gleaming mass. "And your eyes are like the mountains themselves, sometimes amethyst, sometimes gray, always beckoning." Sara's eyes closed beneath the gentle touch of his fingertips. "Your skin is as silken as spring's first rains." His hands slid over her shoulders. "Your breasts just fit my hand, as if made for only my touch."

With her eyes closed, Sara was cut off from everything but the sound of his voice and the feel of his hands on her body. The moan that slid from her throat was as much from the pleasure of his words as the pleasure of his touch. He was making love to her with his voice; every husky word drew her closer to the edge she knew awaited.

His hand slid from her breasts to tangle in the golden curls that guarded her femininity. Her lashes came up, the smoky violet of her eyes meeting the simmering green of his. He seemed to look deep inside, reaching for her very soul. His hands cupped her, his fingers finding the welcoming dampness of her.

"Cody." His name was a mere breath. She couldn't drag her eyes from his, couldn't look away from the flame that drew her closer, promising her a completion she had to have. Their only contact was his hand on that most private part of her. His finger slipped inside and her knees buckled, her breath leaving her in a rush. His free arm caught her around the waist, supporting her as his hand left her without hurry.

Sara's arms came up to circle his neck as he lifted her, cradling her to his chest. Her mouth parted beneath the hunger of his. The warm liquid pressure that centered in her loins was spreading throughout her body. She was clay for him to mold with the touch of his fingers, the strength of his body.

He knelt to place her on one of the sleeping bags, and her lashes fluttered. The naked hunger in her eyes was his undoing. His body throbbed in sweet agony. His vision was filled with her. The rough cave, the storm outside—everything else faded away. Nothing mattered but the two of them.

"Cody." Her hands slid up his arms to his shoulders, drawing him down to her. Her legs shifted, inviting him. Slowly, moving as if she were made of fragile porcelain, he stretched his length along hers, his hips sliding between her thighs.

The heat of him seared its way into her flesh, setting her on fire. Her fingers knotted in his hair as his mouth found hers. She twisted demandingly beneath him, wanting completion, needing to feel him within. She could feel him against her, silk-covered steel, hot and hard. There was a moment when he seemed to test himself against her, and her hips arched. She'd never been so demanding, so wanton. Her hands found the hard muscles of his hips, but he needed no urging.

The hard strength of him slid into the welcoming dampness of her, and Sara felt the delicious friction of the movement from her head to her toes.

Cody's senses swam with pure pleasure. She was so hot around him. She held him as if made for only him. No other woman could fit him so perfectly. His hands slid to her hips, deepening the contact. He wanted to absorb her into himself. He wanted to let the sweet flame of her cleanse him of a lifetime of loneliness. For the first time, he belonged somewhere. Absolutely and forever.

Sara felt as if the fire that burned a few feet away had settled in the pit of her stomach. And each rocking thrust drove the flames higher, consuming her. Her hands moved restlessly up and down Cody's back, searching for something to cling to, something solid to anchor her as the world began to spin around them.

Cody felt the shivering tension in her break loose, felt the way she tightened around him. Her neck arched, her hair spilling over the dark fabric like palest silk. She whispered his name, high and breathless, as if it were the last word she'd ever utter. His fingers tightened on her hips, tilting her to him. His body arched as the fire exploded into a million sparks and he shuddered with completion.

Outside, the sleet fell with relentless persistence. Nature was oblivious to the more-contained storm that had raged so fiercely in the wide cavern. Winter was coming, and this storm was a final warning to the creatures who dwelt in the mountains that they should finish up autumn's business and get ready for the long cold months ahead. If the two humans were too absorbed in each other to heed the warning, that was not the storm's concern.

In the dark warmth of the cave, Sara murmured a protest as Cody lifted himself from her and rolled to the side. "Where are you going?"

"Not far." He slid his arm under her shoulder and drew her against his side. Despite the fire, the air was cool, but neither of them noticed it. The heat that had blazed between them had left a lingering warmth that served as well as any blanket.

"Are you all right?" His hand stroked the damp tendrils of hair back from her forehead, the movement so tender that Sara felt tears come to her eyes. She nodded, turning her head to kiss his palm.

"You know, I saw you at the pool. I knew I had no right to invade your privacy like that, but once I saw you, I couldn't look away."

"I knew you were there." She blushed as his eyes widened. "I wanted to be angry and embarrassed, but all I could think of was that I wished it was your hands on me and not just your eyes."

He groaned. "You shouldn't say things like that. It might get you ravished."

"Promise?" Her eyes met his and she sobered, her fingers touching his cheek. "I'm sorry I hit you."

"I'm not. If you hadn't hit me, we wouldn't have ended up here. I'm sorry you were worried."

"It was just that you seemed to actually be enjoying the storm." The sleet lashed down harder outside. A sudden gust of wind blew cold, wet air into their shelter, and Cody's arms tightened around her, absorbing her shiver with his strength.

"Are you frightened of the storm?"

She shook her head uncertainly. "It's not the storm itself that scares me. It's what it can do. Evan's plane went down in a storm over the Sierras. And now Cullen is out there, and I thought I was going to lose both of you."

She shut her mouth abruptly, frightened of what those words might say about her feelings for this man. If Cody heard the potential in her words, he didn't acknowledge it.

"I've always loved storms," he murmured against her hair. "I was born in the middle of the worst blizzard anyone had seen in years. And I took my first steps during a summer thundershower."

"Where were you born?" Sara asked. His husky voice served to block out thoughts of nature's display outside, and Sara didn't want him to stop talking.

"Cody, Wyoming."

"Is that where you got your name?"

"Uh-huh." His lips teased at the soft curls near her temple.

"What about Wolf? Where does that come from?"

"My great-grandfather was named Brother-to-the-Wolf. As the old traditions died out, my grandfather took the name Wolf."

"So you don't have a tribal name?"

"Not officially. My grandfather didn't want me to lose touch completely with the old ways. He gave me the name Stormwalker when I was a boy. He said it could be my private name." He drew his head back, looking down at her intently. "There are people who feel that the giving of a name is giving a piece of yourself, opening the way for evil spirits, unless the other person has something to give in return."

Sara shook her head uncertainly. "I don't have anything to offer. I'm afraid I can't give you a secret name. All I have is myself."

"Can you offer me that?" His mouth smiled, but something flickered in the back of his eyes, giving the lie to that smile. Beneath her palm, she could feel the steady thud of his heart. Could she offer him herself? It was something she'd given to no one.

"I'm all yours," she whispered. His smile faded. This was too dangerous. Why had he told her his name? Why had he asked her for something in return? The game was too serious. It cut too close to the bone, threatening to reveal things he didn't want to see.

His arms tightened for a moment and then he dropped a kiss on her forehead and rolled away, letting the cold air sweep across her naked body. The chill Sara felt was more than physical, but there was a twinge of relief that went with it. They'd been too close to taking steps neither of them was prepared for.

He stood up, stretching. "The fire is about to go out, and this sleeping bag isn't big enough for two."

Sara watched sleepily as he knelt in front of the fire. The flames cast golden highlights over the copper of his skin, catching in the thick blackness of his hair. He looked like a Remington statue cast in bronze.

He fed the fire, coaxing the flickering flames to life. One of the horses snorted, and he moved to the back of the cavern to lay a soothing hand on the animal's neck, murmuring quietly. He was totally unself-conscious about his nudity. He wasn't flaunting his body. At this moment, in this setting, clothes would have been an intrusion, and he wore his own skin with a grace that few men could manage in designer origi-nals.

Sara had to drag her eyes from the masculine beauty of him. He was right. One sleeping bag was not going to do for both of them. But they could zip both bags together and come up with a comfortable bed.

A few minutes later she was snuggled firmly against Cody's side. Physically they were close, but there was a subtle mental distance between them. Each had re-treated from the other, giving them the space they needed to deal with the sudden changes in their rela-tionship.

They fell asleep without speaking again. Making love had been inevitable. Now that it had happened, it was easy to see how they'd been struggling against it from the beginning. It wasn't possible to regret the step they had taken, but the change was too drastic for either of them to be able to predict the direction in which it might lead them.

The sleet continued to fall, but Sara forced herself to stop thinking about what might be happening with Cullen. The high country had already seen several snowstorms. It wasn't as if this weather would catch him unexpectedly. The best thing she could do for him was to get some sleep so that they could start first thing in the morning.

Cody listened to her breathing grow more shallow and steady, and his arm tightened around her. One slender hand lay against his chest, just over his heart, and he fought the urge to move it, his mouth twisting ruefully. The symbolism was irresistible. But moving her hand wasn't going to save his heart. He had the feeling that it was already cupped in her small palm.

He forced the thought away, making his mind a careful blank. He didn't want to analyze anything tonight. All he wanted was sleep. Perhaps with her at last beside him, the dreams would leave him alone and he could sleep through the night without being haunted by her eyes.

He'd been asleep for some time when the dream came to him. His brows hooked together in silent protest, but he was swept up in the dream pattern. Floating on invisible wings, he looked down on the crash. The plane was a twisted mass of silver and red. Red for blood. But the only wound he could see was the path the plane had gouged out of the land. And this time he could feel pain. Tamped down but vivid. And then that was gone. Swallowed in death? He twisted in protest, fighting the hold of the dream. Not again. He couldn't go through this again. But the dream held him tightly, pulling him, drawing on all his senses until he could have taken the path to the crash with his eyes closed. This was a place to which he had to go. Something he had to do.

And then it was gone as suddenly as it had come. He woke abruptly, a sense of urgency still clinging to him. Beneath the weight of the sleeping bag, his skin was bathed in a film of cold sweat. His heart was pounding as if he'd run the miles that lay between the cave and the broken plane. His hand swept out, seeking the warmth of Sara's slim body. But the bed was empty.

His eyes opened slowly and looked directly into the concerned depths of hers. In the predawn light that filtered into the cave, her eyes were a silver gray to match the sky outside. She crouched beside the fire, carefully feeding in small sticks of wood. The fire licked up around the fuel eagerly, and Cody felt as if it licked his skin. A moment before he had been cold, but now dread swept through him as hot as a burning branding iron.

The look in her eyes told him that she knew he'd been dreaming. But just what did she know? She'd demanded to know how he was going to find the crash site. But did she really want to know?

He'd learned to hide the dreams at an early age. Only his grandfather had understood and accepted them. His mother had looked at him out of worried green eyes, not so much disbelieving as frightened of what the dreams could do to her only child. And his father had been too busy trying to fit into a world that was totally foreign to his ancestors. Too busy to understand a son who would have been a shaman in an earlier time.

Only Cody's grandfather had understood and accepted the dreams as completely natural. A gift from the Great Spirit to be cherished and used carefully. Cody sometimes felt as if they were more a curse than a gift, but he had learned to live with them, accepted them as something that was a part of him. He also learned to conceal them.

And now, here was Sara, watching him from wide gray eyes, questioning, concerned. She'd wrapped herself in his shirt, probably the first thing that had come to hand when she got up. His eyes shifted from hers, avoiding the questions he read there.

"You're up early." He eased out of the sleeping bag and reached for his jeans. Dog looked up from his position near the mouth of the cave, his yellow eyes offering a silent greeting.

"You were dreaming." Cody's fingers froze on the snap of his jeans, but he refused to raise his head.

"Was I?"

"This is the third night in a row that you've talked in your sleep." His head jerked up, his eyes met hers for an instant before sliding away. So she hadn't been asleep those other times. "Twisted silver. You keep mentioning twisted silver." He closed his eyes as the wrecked plane came to him as clearly as if he were standing in front of it.

"Do I?" He bent to slip a larger piece of wood onto the fire.

Sara swallowed hard against the lump in her throat, feeling it settle heavily in her chest. He didn't want to talk about this. But she had to know.

"It's the plane, isn't it? You've seen it in your dreams."

Cody said nothing. He'd never lied about the dreams. He avoided mentioning them, but he never lied if backed into a corner. There was something inside him that felt as if that would taint the dreams. His mouth tasted coppery with fear, but he wouldn't lie to her.

Sara stood up and came around the fire to stand in front of him. "Cody, that's how you know where the crash site is, isn't it?'' Her fingers gripped his forearm, pressing against the muscles as if she could force the truth from him with that pressure. When his eyes at last met hers, they were a bleak and cold green.

''Why do you want to know?''

She blinked. ''Why shouldn't I know? I think it's reasonable that I should want to know how you're going to find Cullen. If you're seeing things in your dreams, I have a right to know what they are.''

His arm knotted beneath her fingertips for an instant before he jerked it away. ''No! No one has a right to know what I dream.''

His anger was such that Sara had to force herself to stay where she was. ''Cody, I don't mean to invade your privacy, but if you've seen something about Cullen, I'd like to know what it is. He's all I have in the world. Please. If you know something, tell me.''

''I don't know anything.'' He half turned away, avoiding the plea in her eyes. The habits were too old, too deeply ingrained to be discarded for a pair of bewitching eyes. He'd been hiding that part of himself for too long.

Sara felt as if she were battering at a brick wall. He knew something and she had to know what it was. She had to know what he'd seen of Cullen.

''I don't believe that. You can't tell me that you haven't dreamed about the crash the last three nights.''

He spun to face her with a suddenness that startled a gasp from her. ''I've been dreaming about that damned crash ever since the plane went down. I woke up the night after it happened with sweat dripping from me. I could hardly breathe. Do you know what fear tastes like?''

The anger that lashed out of him was so intimidating that Sara shook her head, taking a step back. Cody's hand shot out, his long fingers closing around her upper arm. The pressure stopped well short of hurtful, but it was clear that he planned on her staying right where she was.

"It tastes like acid on your tongue. Your chest hurts with the need to breathe and your vision blurs and you want to throw up only you can't because your throat doesn't seem to be working right. That's what I felt in that dream. As if I were in the plane with them, feeling it go down, knowing it was going to crash."

He stopped, as if afraid he'd revealed too much, and his fingers dropped away from her arm. Sara's heart was pounding and she had to swallow hard before she could force her voice out.

"Is he... Are they dead?" The question echoed in the cavern, lingering against the rock walls.

"I don't know. Don't you understand? I don't know anything." The agony in his voice was unmistakable. "If I knew that, I would tell you." His fingers raked through his hair before dropping to his sides and clenching into fists. "All I get is the crash itself. And there's pain." He shuddered, his eyes blank, looking at things she couldn't see. "Then the pain is gone but I don't know if it's because of death or something else."

He shook his head and his eyes refocused on her. She wanted to cry out at the pain she read there. "It's all right. I'm sure they're alive. I'd know if Cullen was dead."

He shook his head as if he hadn't even heard her. "It's just like the other times. I saw the crashes and I had to go and find them. And each time there was nothing but death. I want to believe this one is different, but what if it isn't?''

Sara wrapped her arms around her body, feeling the chill morning air clear to her bones. "If you dreamed the crash right after it happened, why didn't you tell someone where it was?"

His eyes focused on her for a moment and she read resentment in their depths. "Until you arrived, I didn't get anything but the crash. It wasn't until you showed up that something began pulling me toward the site. It was as if everything waited for your arrival."

"Do you know where the plane went down?"

"Not exactly. There's a . . . tugging that pulls me as we go along, but I couldn't pinpoint the place on a map."

"Don't you think that that tugging has to mean that someone is alive? It wouldn't be the same if they were both dead, would it?"

Cody looked into her pleading eyes and hesitated. He could agree with her. What harm would come from that? But it would be offering her a hope that could be false. He shook his head slowly.

"I was pulled to the other crashes, too, and no one survived those. But the other two weren't as strong as this." He offered the last words as the only reassurance he could give.

Sara bit her lip, her eyes shifting away from his as if afraid to reveal her vulnerability. She couldn't believe that Cullen was dead. She had to keep believing that he had survived the crash and would be expecting her to find him.

"Cullen is alive." She said it flatly as if saying it could make it so.

"I hope so."

Her eyes flickered back up to his. "When I asked how you knew where the crash was, why didn't you tell me the truth?"

His brows rose in a sardonic question. "I suppose you would have casually accepted it if I'd told you that I was dreaming our route? People aren't comfortable with that idea. That's why John Larkin was so reluctant to give you my name. He wanted to know how I found the others, and I told him."

"And you just assumed that I would react the same way?" She couldn't keep the hurt from her voice.

Cody looked at her for a long moment, realizing that it wasn't just fear of her reaction that had made him hide the truth from her. The dreams were an intensely private thing, something he kept to himself. Sara Grant had already worked her way deep into his life. Her appearance in his dreams had shown him that she was going to be important somehow. Instinctively, he fought against letting her get any closer than she already had.

Telling her about the dreams was opening a part of himself that he shared with no one. But now that it was out and she was not looking at him as if he were a freak in a sideshow, he felt as if a tremendous burden had fallen from his shoulders. His mouth twisted in a half smile though his eyes remained guarded.

Sara did not resist when he reached out to draw her close, but hurt feelings kept her shoulders stiff, her mouth tight. It was frightening to realize how much it hurt that he'd shut her out, labeling her an outsider in his life. It didn't matter that logic told her that that was exactly what she was. She didn't feel like an outsider and it hurt to be treated like one.

The mat of hair on his chest felt crisp beneath her cheek, and his voice rumbled in her ear. "There aren't very many people who are comfortable with things they don't understand. John Larkin isn't alone. He's a good man, but he doesn't like things that don't come with a cut-and-dried explanation. I've learned that it's best not to tell people things that frighten them."

His hand stroked up and down her back, and Sara felt the tension ease out of her, realizing that he was offering her more of an explanation than she really had a right to expect. She let herself relax against him, telling him without words that she understood.

Cody bent his head over hers, feeling her acceptance sweep over him like a cleansing breeze. He hadn't realized how badly he wanted her to believe in him until now. But along with the relief came fear. She was too close. She meant too much. His hand lifted to tangle in her hair, tilting her head back. His eyes skimmed over the delicate perfection of her features. Emotion brought a tightness to his throat, but he backed away from examining that emotion to closely. Their worlds lay too far apart for him to let her get closer.

Sara's arms came up, her hands burrowing into the shaggy thickness of his hair as his mouth lowered to hers. The kiss they shared was one of healing more than passion.

When he lifted his head, the faint smile on his mouth was reflected in his eyes. "The storm cleared up last night."

Sara turned in his arms to look outside. It couldn't be said that the weather was glorious, but the sleet had stopped and there were even hints of weak sunshine struggling through the clouds.

Dancer shifted restlessly, and Cody gave Sara a quick squeeze before his arms fell away from her. "We'd better get started. I want to try and make up for some of the time the storm cost us yesterday."

The Survivor

CULLEN WINCED as he stumbled over a dip in the ground and jarred his injured leg. Even without the bandage the knee refused to bend, but that didn't stop it from hurting. He steadied himself on the heavy branch he'd whittled into a crude cane.

His watch had been shattered in the crash, but a glance up at the sky told him that he should start looking for a place to camp for the night. A place that could be guarded, he added silently. He didn't have to glance over his shoulder to see the shadowy form that had been trailing him for the past two days. Whether he saw it or not, he knew the coyote was back there. He'd first seen it two mornings ago, and the animal had been trailing along behind him ever since.

His mouth twisted in a humorless smile. Nature had a way of taking care of loose ends. The coyote could scent an injured animal and that was exactly what Cullen was—an injured animal. He was too big for the coyote to risk a direct confrontation with him, but the animal had the patience of a hunter. Sooner or later this strange, two-legged beast would be his. Exhaustion, cold temperature, or his injuries would fell him. It didn't matter to the coyote which it was.

Two hours later, Cullen huddled deeper into his sleeping bag. He was sitting up, his back to a rock overhang, a crackling fire between him and the rest of the world. His right hand lay outside the sleeping bag, the heavy pistol on his good knee. He could doze in this position without falling completely asleep and leaving himself vulnerable. He didn't think it was his imagination that put the occasional stealthy movement into the darkness beyond the firelight.

The temperature was dropping rapidly. Winter was becoming an undeniable fact. The snow was still little more than a shallow covering, but it wouldn't be long before it began to deepen.

He closed his eyes wearily. He wasn't moving fast enough. If he was going to beat winter down out of the mountains, he had to hurry. But with his leg in the condition it was in, every step was a painful effort. And he couldn't afford to risk a fall. He forced his eyes open and added a few more sticks to the fire.

He looked out into the darkness and his nostrils flared. The coyote was out there. Watching, waiting. Confident that, sooner or later, his time would come.

Cullen's lips drew back in a snarl. "Not yet, my friend. Not yet. I'm going to fool you. Because I'm going to get out of here." His quiet words rang with confidence.

He couldn't afford to believe anything else.

Chapter Nine

Sara felt as if her emotions had fallen into two separate compartments. There was the part of her that never stopped worrying about Cullen. Wondering if he was safe, if he was hurt, if he was warm enough. And then there was the part that could think of nothing but Cody. The scent of him, the taste of his skin, the feel of his hands, the smoky sound of his voice.

She felt guilty about being so absorbed in Cody when Cullen's safety was uncertain, but the emotions that Cody drew out in her were too powerful, too driving, for guilt to suppress them. Whether or not she got involved with Cody, it had no effect on Cullen. In her more honest moments she admitted that she had little choice about her relationship with Cody. Like a wildfire that burned out of control, he'd swept aside any feeble barriers she might have put up.

When they left the cave and started on the day's journey, everything was just as it had been for the past few days with one major exception. Dog ranged ahead as he always had, and Cody rode Dancer at the head of their little parade just as he always had, but now Sara rode next to Cody. Dancer and Satin paced side by side, so close that Sara's knee brushed Cody's.

If they each felt the need for a bit of emotional distance, Sara felt an equal need for physical closeness. And Cody obviously didn't object. Once mounted, he turned to look over their little group and, as he faced forward, his eyes caught Sara's studying him. The slow smile that curved his mouth sent a jolt through her and she felt almost mesmerized as he nudged the stallion closer. His long fingers curved around the back of her neck, and she leaned out of the saddle to meet his kiss, as eager for the contact as he was.

Without a word he drew away, his eyes lingering on the swollen softness of her mouth. It seemed an effort for him to force his gaze away from her. His heel tapped Dancer's barrel and the bay obediently started forward. They rode for almost an hour in silence. There didn't seem to be any need for words.

Sara let her thoughts roam without conscious direction. The events of the night before were foremost in her thoughts, but she refused to examine them too closely. Her feelings for Cody were too new and too frightening. She wasn't quite ready to face them in the sharp light of day. Her cheeks flushed with the memory of their lovemaking, and she could only hope that Cody's unusual gifts did not extend to mind reading.

Their physical union had been extraordinarily satisfying. Looking back, Sara blushed at thoughts of her behavior. She'd not only accepted his demands, she'd made demands of her own. He'd delved deep and tapped a vein of sensuality she hadn't even known existed. Certainly David had never brought out that explosive passion.

David. Some of the remembered glow faded from her eyes. Just where did David fit in now? He'd been the farthest thing from her mind last night. In fact, she hadn't really thought about him since meeting Cody Wolf. She closed her eyes for a moment, trying to conjure up David's image. But it was faded and blurred around the edges, like an old, out-of-focus print. Her eyes snapped open and her gloved hands tightened on the reins. Satin hesitated a moment and Sara loosened her grip, letting the mare set the pace necessary to hold them next to Dancer.

David. Dear, sweet David. He was the first photographer she'd worked with, and his patience and encouragement had been a major impetus to her career.

A year ago she and David had moved from being friends to being lovers. There'd been no fireworks, no long soul searching. It had seemed a natural progression in their relationship. And a month ago he'd asked her to marry him. She loved David. She didn't doubt that, and in her more logical moments, she couldn't figure out why she had put off his marriage proposal. He was one of the sweetest men she'd ever met. He loved her. He loved Cullen. Why on earth was she hesitating?

But there'd been something inside that kept her from saying yes. Something that insisted that there had to be more to marriage than the gentle love she felt for David. There should be excitement, fire. Fire. That described her feelings for Cody Wolf perfectly. When he touched her, he set her ablaze. Her mouth twisted. She'd found the fire that was missing with David. Now, all she had to do was see that it didn't consume her.

Cody glanced at his silent companion and his mouth tightened. Her eyes were fixed ahead, but he didn't think she was seeing anything that lay in front of her. Her gaze was focused inward, on things he couldn't see. He'd been afraid that she might want to poke and prod and examine their relationship from every angle. He'd dreaded that she might ask questions he wasn't yet ready to even hear, let alone give answers to. But now that she rode beside him so silently, he found himself irritated by her silence.

"You're thinking about him, aren't you?"

Sara blinked, snapping out of her reverie to focus on Cody. "Cullen? Not consciously."

"The man in Los Angeles."

"What!"

Sara's fingers tightened so suddenly that Satin danced sideways in confusion. Sara loosened her grip and leaned forward to murmur a few words of apology to the mare as they fell back in beside Cody.

Her eyes met his, but she could read nothing in those guarded green depths. The brim of his hat shadowed his face, making it impossible to judge his expression with any accuracy.

"What are you talking about?"

His eyes slanted toward her. "There is a man in Los Angeles, isn't there?"

She hesitated a long moment before nodding slowly. "Yes. But I've never mentioned him. How did you know about him?"

"Nothing mystical. I've seen you carefully taking your birth control pill every morning."

Sara flushed, irritated and embarrassed. Was there nothing he missed seeing? "Maybe I just like to be prepared." There was a distinct snap to her voice.

Cody didn't even have the grace to pretend to consider the matter. He shook his head, his eyes focused ahead. "Not you. If you're taking precautions, it's because you've got a reason for it. Why do you think I didn't ask about it last night? Did you think I would make love to you if I hadn't known you were protected?''

She blinked, and the color in her cheeks deepened until she felt as if her face were on fire. Now that he mentioned it, she hadn't even wondered about that. She'd like to think it was because she knew she was safe from pregnancy. Of course she'd have thought of it otherwise. That's what she wanted to believe. But there was a nagging little voice that suggested that last night she hadn't cared about anything but the feel of his body.

"I hadn't really thought about it," she muttered. She tugged her hat lower with one gloved hand and tried to pretend that the conversation was ended. Maybe he would take the hint.

"Were you thinking about him?" His tone was one of casual inquiry, but Sara had the feeling that he wasn't going to let the subject drop without getting an answer.

"As a matter of fact, I was thinking of him. Is that what you wanted to hear?"

His worn leather jacket creaked with the movement of his shoulders as he shrugged. "What's he like?"

As soon as the words were out of his mouth, he wished he could call them back. Not only were they an intrusion into her privacy, but he didn't want to hear the answer anyway. He'd been struggling against admitting his anger from the first moment he'd realized that she was taking birth control pills. An illogical, unreasonable anger that ate at his gut. Last night had pushed the flames of that anger even higher.

He hated the thought of another man touching her. The intensity of that feeling told him more than anything else that he was getting in too deep. She'd entwined herself into his emotions in a way that no one else had ever managed.

"I'm sorry. That's none of my business."

"No, it isn't. My life before I met you is only my concern."

"You're right. I had no right to ask."

"Then why did you?"

Dancer sidled uneasily in answer to the tension in Cody's hands. Silence lay heavily between them and Sara thought he was going to ignore the question. When he spoke his voice was level, but she could hear strain in the husky tones.

"I guess there's a masochistic streak in me that I've never noticed before." He didn't look at her and Sara could read nothing in his profile.

"Does it bother you to think of me with David?" she probed.

"It makes me want to kill him." His tone was so even, almost casual, that it took her a moment to realize what he'd said. Before she could respond—and what would she have said?—Cody drew Dancer to a halt and nodded to the right.

"We're going to have to go up there."

Sara dragged her eyes from his face, wishing that he wasn't quite so good at concealing his feelings. But their conversation slid to the back of her mind when she saw what he was indicating. To their left the mountains eased into a shallow valley; riding through it would be smooth and easy—the biggest danger was the possibility of a horse putting a foot in a rabbit hole.

To their right the mountain rose abruptly, as if it had its roots in the little valley. The "there" that Cody was indicating was a narrow path that wound up the side of the mountain. From where she sat, Sara thought that

the path looked as if it might have room for a very
small mountain goat, but that it certainly wouldn't give
enough support to allow four horses and two humans
and a large dog to travel on it.

She swallowed hard. "Are you sure?"

"I'm sure." Cody studied her suddenly-pale face for
a moment before offering her a way out. "If you don't
want to try it, you could camp right here while I go on.
We've got enough supplies to split them up."

She was already shaking her head. "I'm going with
you."

He shrugged. "It's up to you." He swung his leg over
the saddle and slid off Dancer's back. "We'll eat some
lunch here. I want to make sure everything is secure
before we tackle that path."

Sara slipped out of the saddle and moved to help him
with the noon meal, trying not to look at the trail they
would be taking later. Her appetite was nonexistent,
and she surreptitiously fed most of her lunch to Dog,
who didn't look at all worried about what was coming
up.

"That's easy for you to say. There's enough room
for you up there. Just what am I supposed to do?" Dog
blinked at her silently, his long pink tongue licking the
last traces of baked beans from his nose. His tail moved
in acknowledgment of her words, but he didn't make
any other contribution to the conversation.

A few yards away, Cody was carefully checking the
packs on all the animals, making sure that everything
was snug. Sara watched him, envying his apparent
calm. As far as she could see, he wasn't at all uneasy
about attempting a climb that would have made Spi-
derman think twice. She glanced at the mountain and
squared her jaw. If that was the way to get to Cullen,

she'd get through it. Even if she had to do it on her hands and knees.

It seemed as if hardly any time at all had passed before their short lunch stop was over and Cody was saying that it was time to start again. He stood next to Satin, and Sara hoped her expression didn't mirror the terror she felt. Some of her feelings must have shown in her eyes, because his hand slid into the soft hair at the base of her neck, stopping her move to put her foot in the stirrup. Sara lifted her eyes to his reluctantly. She didn't want him to see the fear she was trying so hard to control.

"Let Satin choose the path. Keep your hands on the reins, though. She may need you to help her balance. I'll go up first and take the packhorses. If you see me get into any trouble, just stop and wait. Make sure you don't crowd the packhorses. The last thing we need is one of them getting nervous."

Sara nodded, swallowing the knot of fear that threatened to choke her. He'd pushed his hat back off his head, letting it hang down his back. His eyes gleamed emerald in the cloud-muted daylight. He studied her face for a long moment and then his hand slid deeper into her hair until she could feel the faint roughness of callused fingertips against her scalp.

"There's plenty of room on the trail. I've gone up places a lot worse and so have the horses. Just trust your horse and stay calm."

She nodded again, trying to look as if she believed him—trying to look as if her legs weren't trembling with sheer terror. She was not completely successful. Cody's mouth quirked in a tender smile and his other hand came up to stroke her soft cheek.

"Trust me. I wouldn't let you do it if I thought it was too dangerous." He looked into her eyes, which seemed to reflect the cloudy gray sky above them. "You trust me, don't you?" Sara nodded. She trusted him. It was the mountain she didn't trust.

"I wouldn't get you into anything I didn't know you could handle." His head dipped and her eyes closed, her mouth softening in invitation. The kiss was not the quick gesture of reassurance she had been expecting. His mouth slanted over hers as if he were famished for the taste of her. She lifted her hands to his face, as much for the pleasure of touching him as for balance.

His mouth plundered hers of every sweet secret. Tasting, demanding. Teasing a passionate response from her. All thoughts of the climb ahead of them spun out of her mind as she leaned into his body, letting him support her, losing herself in the swirling magic of his kiss.

She murmured an incoherent protest, her palms tightening on the stubble of his beard as he lifted his head. He smiled down into her dazed eyes.

"Concentrate on that instead." Her hands fell to her sides, leaving the only contact between them the explosive meeting of their eyes and his hands in her hair. "And think about tonight?"

"Tonight?" She couldn't drag her eyes from his.

"Tonight I'm going to make love to you until you taste me with every breath you take. Until my scent is imprinted on your skin." Sara's lashes brushed her cheeks as he bent to taste the sensitive skin beneath her ear. "I can't wait to feel your skin against mine." His breath skimmed across her ear. "Your legs wrapped around mine, your body tight around me."

"Cody." Sara hardly knew whether she was protesting his blunt words or begging him to take her there and then. She didn't think she was imagining the reluctance in his movements as he slowly drew away from her, leaving her standing on knees that showed a distinct tendency to wobble.

"Up you go." She accepted his boost into the saddle without a word. She wasn't sure she could have forced a word out, even if she'd known what to say. She couldn't drag her eyes away from his long-legged stride as he crossed the few yards to where Dancer stood. He swung up into the saddle, and she found herself noticing the way the soft denim molded his thighs, remembering the feel of those hard muscles under her hands.

They were well on their way up the narrow trail before she remembered to be frightened.

Unfortunately, once she remembered, the fright returned with a vengeance. The trail was so narrow that her right boot brushed against the cliff face and, at times, her left boot was hanging out over a sheer drop that seemed to increase logarithmically with every step the mare took. After one look downward, she jerked her eyes up and kept them fixed firmly on Cody's back. It was just as well that he'd told her to let the mare find her own way, because Sara didn't think she could have managed a single coherent action on her own. All she could do was cling to the reins and mutter one childhood prayer after another.

Telling herself that this was the only way to get to Cullen braced her mentally, but it didn't do anything for the sick knot that had lodged itself in the pit of her stomach. Was it possible to get car sick on the back of a horse? Well, she could hardly stop and take a Dramamine.

She risked another glance down and then wished she hadn't. She couldn't imagine the valley looking any farther away if she'd been looking at it from the moon. She dragged her eyes back to the solid bulk of Cody's back. She didn't even dare to look ahead to the end of the trail.

Ahead of her, one of the packhorses stumbled as a hoof came down too close to the rocky edge. Sara's breath caught on a sob as she watched the animal scramble frantically. For a moment it looked as if the battle would be lost, and she waited to see the horse plunge to its death. She was hardly aware of her hands' tightening on the reins, pulling Satin to a halt, leaving plenty of room between them and the potential disaster a few feet away.

Cody turned in his saddle but he was helpless to do anything to aid the struggling animal. He'd tied the animals together in such a way that if one of them fell the knots would slip loose, preventing the others from being dragged over the side. But he'd raised this horse from a foal and he would feel its loss.

With a frightened snort, the horse lunged forward, scrabbling frantically for a moment until it managed to get all four feet under it. Cody's voice floated back to Sara as he spoke soothingly to the trembling animal. The incident had sent a ripple of terror through all four horses. She could feel Satin tensing beneath her and she leaned forward to whisper to the mare, stroking the taut neck with her free hand. The immediate danger had passed, but they stayed where they were for several long moments.

Suspended between heaven and earth, Sara had never been so aware of her own mortality as she was then. It could have been Satin who'd stumbled, and she might not have recovered. Sara closed her eyes, offering up a silent prayer of thanks.

She opened her eyes and looked over the mare's head, her eyes colliding with Cody's. At this distance she couldn't see the expression in his eyes, but the impact of his gaze was as powerful as ever. He seemed to stare at her intently for a long, silent moment before he lifted his hand, thumb up, in the universal signal of triumph. She returned the gesture, hoping he wouldn't be able to see that her hand was shaking.

The rest of the climb was uneventful, if she didn't count the fact that she never knew at what point Satin might slip and send the two of them hurtling over the side of the mountain. She watched Cody and Dancer, followed by the packhorses, disappear around a curve. When she rounded the curve, she saw that the last few feet of the trail were almost straight up. Helpless to do anything else, she closed her eyes, feeling Satin's muscles tighten as the mare gathered herself. The mare lunged suddenly upward and Sara's eyes flew open, expecting to see the two of them hurtling into space. But before Sara had a chance to do more than mutter a succinct prayer, Satin had scrambled up onto solid ground.

Dog was sitting a few feet from the edge, his expression as bland as ever. The climb hadn't been a problem for him. If she'd had the strength, Sara would have slid from the saddle and kissed the sweet earth beneath them. But once down, she knew she'd never make it back onto the horse, so she contented herself with a shaky smile.

"Are you okay?"

"Sure. Never better. Piece of cake." The quick pressure of his hand over hers told her that he didn't believe her breezy reassurances for a moment, but it also conveyed his admiration. Sara's smile steadied a bit.

Though they rode side by side for the rest of the afternoon, their conversation was rather desultory. It was some time before Sara could even trust her voice to hold up. When she finally spoke, she didn't bring up the close call on the trail. That was too new, too fresh in her mind. She wanted to forget it.

"What kind of things do you do on your ranch?"

"Things?" Cody glanced at her, one dark brow hooking a question above his eyes.

"Things. You know. Do you raise cows or horses or gerbils, or what?"

One side of his mouth twisted in a half smile. "It's cattle, not cows. And I'd like to admit that I have the West's first gerbil ranch but I'm afraid it's nothing that innovative. I raise horses. Quarter horses. I'm trying to build a reputation as the best place to go to get a good working horse. And Dancer here is going to help with that." He leaned forward to pat the stallion's neck, and Dancer bobbed his head as if in acknowledgment of the words.

"Have you always lived on the ranch?"

"Not always. My grandfather left it to me. He lived there a good part of his life. I used to spend summers here, but my father wanted to fit in with the White Man's world so we lived in Denver, Cheyenne, Laramie, or wherever he could find work."

"You sound bitter."

"Bitter? No. I got over that a long time ago. He was never very happy. He was too much Comanche to deny his heritage completely and too afraid of it to accept it completely. It's not a comfortable way to live."

"What about you? Are you comfortable with your heritage?" He was silent for so long that Sara was afraid she'd overstepped some unseen bounds and offended him.

"Comfortable is not a word that I associate with myself. I've come to terms with what it means to be half Comanche, half white. I try to take some of the good from each and mold them into something workable. The army was one of the best things that happened to me."

"When were you in the army?" Her eyes skimmed over him, trying to imagine him in uniform, trying to imagine him conforming to someone else's rules.

His eyes met hers, and she read the faint amusement in them, as if he could read her thoughts. "I joined when I got out of high school. There didn't seem to be much else for me to do. No money for college, no money for anything else. My parents were both dead by then, and my grandfather could barely scrape a living for himself out of the ranch. I spent one summer living like a bum in Denver. I drank heavily and chain-smoked and generally made a fool of myself. I had a real chip on my shoulder about being a Native American. I got thrown into jail one night for stealing a car. I hadn't done it but I knew the guys who had. Luckily, they were stupid enough to get caught with the evidence and the police let me out.

"It sobered me up, though. Another couple of months and it could have been me who'd stolen the car. That was the direction I was headed. I hitchhiked from

Denver to the ranch. I think I wanted some comfort, a shoulder to cry on, but my grandfather took one look at me and threw me in the horse tank." He laughed softly at the memory.

"He told me that I wasn't setting foot in the house until I smelled like a man and not a wine bottle. He made me sleep in the barn for a solid week and he worked my butt off every day. When he finally decided that I was fit to enter the house, he sat me down at the table and slapped an ad for the military down in front of me, and said that he was damned if he was going to see me become another statistic to add to the high rate of teen suicide and alcoholism among Indians."

"And you joined up, just like that?"

"I argued, but I knew he was right. What else could I do? I joined the army."

"I bet he was proud of you."

"I suppose so. He died while I was serving my second tour in Vietnam." He ignored her involuntary gasp. "He left me the ranch and just enough cash to pay the taxes."

"It must have been awful for you."

"Oh, I don't know. Grandfather always felt that the Great Spirit had a reason for everything he did. The army taught me how to work within the system, how to twist it to my own ends. I knew I wanted to raise horses, just as he and I had always talked about, but that would take money, and to get money I had to have an education. So I used the GI bill to go to college and get a business degree, and then I joined an investment firm."

"An investment firm?" If she'd had a hard time picturing him in a uniform, it was even more difficult to imagine him in a three-piece suit.

"You know—when E. F. Hutton talks, people listen—that kind of thing. I figured out how much money I'd have to have to get started, and then I began investing every dime I could lay my hands on. I lucked out and developed a flair for that kind of thing. It took about five years, but I gathered together what I needed and quit."

"Weren't you tempted to stay? I mean, you had all the comforts of civilization. If you were doing well, you probably could have made a fortune."

He was shaking his head even before she'd finished speaking. "I didn't want the comforts of civilization. Not if it meant giving up this." His hand swept out to encompass the mountains that surrounded them. "I think I'm too much the Comanche to ever be happy living in the city."

His eyes met hers, and she could read his burning love of freedom for an instant before he seemed to become aware of just how much he was revealing. Then that one glimpse into his soul was over, and the smile he gave her was slightly forced.

"There's something about you that makes me say more than I intend to when I open my mouth."

"Maybe it's because you trust me." She was daring a lot, perhaps pushing too far, too fast, but the words were out before she could change her mind. She met his searching look openly, unable to read anything in the enigmatic green depths of his.

"Maybe." And that one word clearly closed the conversation.

They made camp just before dark. Cody pitched the tent in a corner formed where a low ridge met the bulk of the mountain, providing them with some shelter from the cold wind that had picked up in the afternoon. A fire was always welcome, but never more so than tonight. The temperature had dropped to a near bone-chilling level, and Sara found herself huddling as close to the fire as she could get without setting fire to her clothing. Even Dog seemed to welcome the extra warmth, and he stayed near the camp, graciously sharing their evening rations.

After the meal, Cody went to make one last check on the horses while Sara crawled into the tent. He'd placed their sleeping bags in the tent but he hadn't zipped them together, and she hesitated for a moment, surprised. Was he trying to tell her something, or was he just being careful not to assume too much? She tossed the question around in her mind for a few minutes before zipping the two bags together with a defiant toss of her head.

Nothing ventured, nothing gained, she told herself firmly. If Cody didn't want to sleep with her, he could come right out and say it. After what they'd shared the past few days, coy behavior had no part in their relationship.

Cody's footsteps slowed as he stepped into the firelight and realized that Sara was already in the tent. He banked the fire for the night, so that there would be hot coals to ease starting it again in the morning. He rubbed his hand over Dog's rough coat, murmuring a few quiet words to him. He was only putting off the inevitable.

When he ducked into the tent, he wasn't sure what he hoped to see. He wanted Sara. Last night had only whetted his appetite for her. But it would be safer to back off now while there was still time. He'd left the decision up to her. If she didn't want to sleep with him, she had only to let the sleeping bags remain apart.

Sara looked up as he entered the tent. She'd lit a lantern and set it at the back of the small enclosure, and the clear light of it turned her fine hair into a halo. She was sitting up in the middle of the zipped-together sleeping bags, carefully rubbing lotion into her slender hands.

Cody hesitated a moment as their eyes met. Her eyes were lavender again tonight, reflecting the color of the flannel shirt she was wearing. He wanted to drag his gaze from hers and turn and leave the tent. He wanted to prove that he could walk away from her. He sank to his knees on one corner of the sleeping bag.

"Do you always take such good care of your hands?" He tried not to notice how hypnotic her motions were as she smoothed the cream into her arms.

"I have to. No one wants a hand model with red, chapped hands." She capped the bottle of lotion and set it aside. Out of the corner of her eye, she could see him unbuttoning his shirt. If was appalling how that simple movement affected her pulse rate. She rose on her knees to set the lotion next to her clothing, giving herself a few seconds to steady her pulse. But when she turned back, he was right there.

He knelt in front of her, naked to the waist, tanned skin stretched over rippling muscles. She lifted her head slowly, meeting his eyes, half afraid that she might drown in the fiery green depths of them.

His fingers came up to tangle in the silk of her hair, and she melted against his chest, hungry for the feel of him. Her hands slid into the shaggy thickness of his hair, pulling his head down to hers. Their lips met.

His hands were impatient with the buttons on her shirt, and her fingers shook over the fastening of his jeans. There was so much heat. She would surely burn unless she could feel his skin against hers. But when the smooth coppery weight of him pressed her back onto their bed, she learned the true meaning of heat.

His mouth closed over her breast. Her fingers bit into the lean muscles of his hips. She twisted beneath him. And then the fire of him was deep within her. A half sob, a guttural moan. A completion.

As if she were a match and he was the flame, Sara burned for him. If his hands were bruising on her hips, her nails dug into his shoulders. The hunger was too intense, too explosive to last long. She arched beneath him, drawing a low groan from him as her body tightened around him, dragging him into the vortex of her climax.

The storm receded slowly, leaving them spent. Cody's hands shook as he shifted her awkwardly, easing both of them beneath the heavy weight of the upper sleeping bag. Sara had only enough strength left to snuggle up against him, throwing her arm across his sweat-dampened chest, her leg across the solid muscles of his thighs.

Somewhere a coyote howled, a long moaning wail that echoed off the mountains. Dog growled low in his throat but he didn't lift his head from his paws. An owl hooted mournfully and small creatures scurried for cover as the dark shadow passed over the ground.

Inside the tent Cody turned off the lantern, letting the darkness outside take over. Burying his face in the scented warmth of Sara's hair, he let himself drift to sleep. With her slight weight against him, it seemed as if all was right with the world.

The Survivor

THE COYOTE WAS GETTING more bold. He no longer bothered to skulk quite so far back. Cullen found that he even admired the animal's persistence in a funny way. He only wished that he weren't the object of its attention.

He settled back against the rock wall where he'd made camp and dug through his frighteningly empty pack for something to eat. Coming up with a can of sardines, he grimaced faintly. He hated sardines. A few minutes later he drank the oily juices from the empty can, feeling the fish ease the knot of hunger from his stomach.

He leaned his head back on the rock and closed his eyes. The weak sunshine lit the hollows and shadows of his face. Pain had drawn deep lines in his face, making him look much older than his eighteen years. He lifted one hand to explore the healing cut along the side of his face. It itched and he had to resist the urge to scratch.

Sensing that he was no longer alone, he opened his eyes and stared straight into yellow irises, watching him with the detached interest a researcher might show for a rat. For a long moment, the man and the coyote stared at each other. Barely ten yards separated them, and Cullen could see muscles shift beneath a shaggy winter coat as the animal moved.

For just an instant, there was a part of him that wanted to close his eyes and go to sleep and let the coyote win. He was so tired of struggling. It would be so pleasant to just fall asleep, to shut out the throbbing pain in his leg, to forget the sound of screaming metal and the rattle of Bill's breathing just before it stopped forever.

To just give up and sleep.

The thought was so frightening that he jerked himself upright, the movement sending a stabbing jolt of pain through his knee. But the pain was welcome. It made him realize that he was alive and determined to stay that way. The coyote's eyes met his again and the animal seemed to realize that his time had not yet come. He turned and trotted off, disappearing around a boulder. But Cullen knew he'd be back.

Chapter Ten

The dreams continued to haunt Cody, but he found they were easier to deal with now that Sara knew about them. For the first time in his life, he had someone to share the terror with. The higher they climbed, the more vivid the images grew. Logic told him that the chance of there being any survivors was slim, but he continued to hope. And Sara never gave up her determination that Cullen was alive.

There was a feeling of companionship between them, which Sara had known only with her brother and her nephew, and Cody had never found before. Even with his grandfather, there had been an open gap between them. No matter how hard they had tried, nothing could change the fact that the world his grandfather had known was nothing like the world Cody faced. Love, respect, admiration—all these emotions had been there, but the two men hadn't been companions in the true sense of the word.

But if Cody's and Sara's days were spent as friends, their nights were spent as lovers. Cody taught Sara that her body could respond to the lightest touch of his finger, and she taught him that physical love was infinitely more satisfying when combined with mental rapport.

He worried about what was going to happen if nothing but death lay at the end of their journey, and despite her insistence that she'd know if Cullen were dead, he sometimes caught a lost, frightened look in her eyes and he knew she was afraid of what they might find.

He woke up one bitterly cold morning, his heart pounding from the aftermath of a dream. Sara slept against his side, her small hand curved into a soft fist on his chest. His arm tightened convulsively around her and she stirred, mumbling in her sleep before settling back into sleep.

Today they would reach the crash site. He knew that as clearly as if it were written on the walls of the tent. What would they find? What if it was like the others—nothing but death and ruin? How would Sara face that?

As if in answer to his mood, the weather was bitterly cold. Winter had been threatening for days, but it had arrived now. The clouds were heavy with snow, which fell in sullen fits and starts, making the footing miserable and slowing their pace to a crawl.

Sara watched Cody, trying to read his mood, but there was nothing to be seen in the impassive line of his profile. He met her occasional remarks with monosyllables, and several times he didn't seem to hear her at all. She had to force herself not to probe. When he wanted to tell her what was wrong, she would listen.

Late in the morning, the path they took began to climb higher, the horses laboring to find solid footing on the sloping trail. Their breath came in gusting clouds of white steam. Sara clung to the saddle, trying not to interfere with Satin's labor as the mare lunged up the steep path. They topped out on a narrow plateau, bordered along the opposite edge by a band of mournful-looking pines. The horses walked tiredly toward the trees.

"Sara..." Cody's voice was raw, and she turned in her saddle, feeling her heart stop at the agonized expression in his eyes.

"What's wrong?"

He shook his head. "Nothing. I..." Dancer came to a halt and Satin stopped beside him. Cody's eyes left hers, and his face tightened as he looked ahead of them.

Sara didn't dare to move. She didn't have to have dreams to know what she was going to see when she turned around. She felt as if she were made of wood, her whole body stiff with tension, as she slowly eased around in the saddle until she looked out over Satin's head.

Below them was a shallow slope, strewn with trees. Beyond that was a continuation of the plateau, mountains looming up around it and throwing dark shadows across the light coating of snow. Halfway across the valley was the plane. Silver and red gleamed through the powdery snow. The metal was twisted; the landing gear pointed up to the sky.

"Oh, my God." The words were half a prayer, half a curse. Her stomach clenched in agony. For the first time, she realized just how slim the chances were that Cullen had survived the crash. Nothing could have lived through the cataclysm that had crumpled the little plane like so much discarded foil.

She didn't even look at Cody as she dug her heels into Satin's side and started down the slope. He didn't speak until they were out of the trees and level with the crash. Then his hand came out to catch hers, drawing the mare to a halt. He had to shake her hand slightly to get her to look at him and his heart twisted at the broken look in her eyes.

"Sara. Let me go on ahead. There's no reason for you to see what might be there."

She shook her head. "I've come this far. I'll go the rest of the way."

He wanted to argue, wanted to insist that she stay behind, but he could read the determination that lay behind her terror. He released his hold on the reins and urged Dancer forward.

If Sara had hoped that the crash might not look quite so bad close up, she was disappointed. The closer she got, the worse it looked. The snow was pristine white and undisturbed, a vivid contrast to the torn metal of the plane. They rode up to within a few yards of the plane and Cody urged the horses around the twisted tail. Cody found himself muttering ancient prayers that he'd half forgotten his grandfather teaching him. He knew from bitter experience just what they could find. Nature was efficient, but she was not always kind.

It seemed as if his prayers were answered when they came to the other side of the plane. At least there were no bodies, no pathetically torn figures strewn in the snow.

They both saw it at the same moment. A long, low mound in the earth, covered with rocks. Sara's breath exploded from her in a sob as the meaning of that mound sank in. A grave. That meant there had been a survivor. Two men. One dead. But which?

She dropped the reins and swung her leg over the saddle, half falling off her horse. Her knees threatened to give way, but she ignored their trembling weakness as she stumbled over the rough ground.

Cody cursed and swung off Dancer's back, letting the reins fall to the ground, knowing the stallion would stay where he'd been left. Sara had fallen to her knees beside the grave and was tearing at the rocks with almost maniacal strength. He called her name but she didn't hear him over the sound of her own sobbing. It wasn't until he grabbed her shoulders and forced her to look at him that she seemed to even remember his existence.

The wild look in her eyes terrified him. Looking at her was like looking into the face of a madwoman. She barely acknowledged his presence before she tried to pull away and return to her clawing attack on the rocks.

"Sara!" He made his voice sharp, trying to penetrate the wall of hysteria that he could feel building between them.

"I have to know. I have to know who it is. Don't you understand? I have to know!"

Emotion lent her slender body strength, and Cody found himself fighting her every step of the way as he dragged her to her feet and forced her away from the grave. She struggled frantically, aware of him only as a barrier to her goal.

"Sara!" He shook her roughly until her eyes snapped into focus and the hysteria receded to lurk at the edges of her gaze.

"I have to know, Cody." The words ended on a sob, and he drew her to him, pressing her face to the cold leather of his jacket for a moment.

"I know you do, honey. I know. But let me do it." She didn't protest as he led her over to a rock that sat in the shadow of the plane and sat her down. "Let me do it."

He brushed his thumb across her cheeks before turning away. He began to move the rocks from the top of the grave with methodical care, stacking them next to the dirt mound. When Sara's gloved hands reached forward to take a stone from his hands, he raised his head to study her face for a long moment before releasing the granite. Fear still screamed in her eyes, but her face was tight with control.

The two of them worked at uncovering the grave without a word. The clouds continued to hover on the shoulders of the mountains, threatening them with snow that didn't quite fall. The wind that blew across the plateau was bitterly cold, whipping the heat from their bodies.

When the last stone had been removed and the dirt-covered mound lay open in front of them, Cody stood up, dusting the dirt from his hands. Sara stared down at the grave as if trying to penetrate the final covering, terrified of what she might see. But she didn't resist when Cody wrapped his fingers around her upper arm and pulled her away. She stumbled on the uneven ground, her eyes blind.

"You stay here while I finish the job." She didn't argue as he went to one of the packhorses and unlashed a pack, searching its contents for the small shovel he'd brought.

She sat on the ground because her legs didn't want to hold her anymore. She was vaguely aware of Cody's moving away and then of the sound of the shovel digging into the dirt. She wanted to shut out the sound of that digging. She wanted to shut out everything. Dog came over and sat down beside her, and the look in his yellow eyes seemed to offer sympathy. With a muffled sob, she threw her arms around his sturdy shoulders and buried her face in the thick fur at his neck. He stood firm, letting her draw what comfort she could from the solid warmth of his body.

Sara didn't cry. The fear had gone too deep for tears. She couldn't even offer up prayers. All she could do was listen to the sound of Cody's shovel and try not to think about what he might uncover. It seemed as if days went by before she heard his soft footfall and knew that he stood next to her. She felt his hand on her head and she stopped breathing, afraid to look up, afraid to move.

"It's not Cullen."

The words echoed strangely in her ears. It wasn't Cullen. Cullen had survived the crash. Her shoulders began to shake and then Cody's arms were around her and she was held close to his strength.

"It's so awful." The words were muffled against his shoulder. He said nothing, brushing his hand over the softness of her hair, absorbing the force of her sobs. "I didn't want it to be Cullen. I couldn't stand to think that it might be Cullen. It's like I wished Bill dead."

"Hush. That's not true." His fingers tangled in her hair, drawing her face back, forcing her to meet his eyes. "You didn't wish anyone dead. What happened here happened weeks ago and it had nothing to do with you. You wouldn't be human if you didn't hope that it wasn't Cullen in that grave."

She nodded uncertainly. With his eyes staring into hers so intently, it was impossible to do anything but agree with him. "What happened to Bill? Can you tell?"

Cody shook his head. "He can't have lived long after the plane crash. It looks like his injuries were pretty massive. I doubt if he even regained consciousness."

Her eyes skimmed past him to the grave site, and she blinked back tears. Bill Taylor had been a friend of Evan's, and though Sara had never known him well, he'd been a part of her life almost as long as she could remember.

"He was a good man."

"Then remember him that way. I'm going to cover the grave again. There's nothing we can do for him now." He glanced up at the cloudy sky. "Look, it's about time for lunch. Don't tell me you can't eat. This isn't the end of the trail for us. You've got to keep up your strength."

Sara swallowed her protest and nodded. He was right. Cullen had survived the crash, but he wasn't here now. They still had to find him. While Cody covered the grave again, Sara heated soup over a small fire, trying not to think about what he was doing.

They ate the soup in silence. There didn't really seem to be anything to say. After the meal, Sara was so emotionally drained that she could only sit next to the fire and stare at the flames. She had been battered back and forth between hope and despair so many times that she no longer knew which emotion dominated.

Cody was worried about her silence, but he left her alone, letting her cope with what had happened in her own way. He climbed into the wrecked plane, hoping to find some sign of what might have happened, but the tangle of wires and dials told him nothing. With a shrug, he jumped out of the cockpit. Machinery had always defeated him. If it had four legs, chances were he could figure out what to do with it, but engines and electronics meant less than nothing.

Sara still sat beside the fire, Dog's huge bulk settled next to her, and after a moment's hesitation, Cody struck off away from the plane. Cullen Grant had obviously survived the crash, and just as obviously had left the wreck. Maybe he'd decided to try and make his way out on foot. Sara said that the boy knew survival. He should have left some indication of direction for any rescuers who might show up.

Cody had exchanged his moccasins for boots, which dealt with the snowfall more comfortably, and their hard soles crunched on the powdery snow. His eyes skimmed the ground for some clue, but unless the boy had taken off only a day or two before, the snow would cover any tracks he might have made. And something told him it had been more than a couple of days since Cullen abandoned the wreckage.

He quartered back and forth across the plateau. When he found it the surge of relief was so tremendous he almost shouted out loud. Even under the snow the shape was clear, and when he bent down to brush the snow away, the stone arrow stood out sharply. He turned to study the direction in which the arrow pointed and then glanced back up at the sky. There was a storm building. It might hold off for several days, or it might break in a matter of hours, but whenever it hit it was going to dump a lot of snow in the high country.

If Cullen was still alive, they had to get to him as quickly as possible and hightail it down out of the Rockies. If Cullen was still alive. A lot could happen to a man alone in the wilderness. A lot depended on his skill and sheer stupid luck. How badly had he been hurt in the crash? What did he have by way of supplies?

Cody shook his head and headed back to the plane. He'd have to take a page out of Sara's book and just believe that the boy was alive.

THEY TRAVELED until almost dark, leaving the wreckage of the plane and Bill's grave behind. Sara was silent, and looking into her face, Cody decided that she was suffering from mild shock. He didn't think it had even sunk in yet that Cullen had been alive when he walked away from the crash.

She ate whatever he put in her hands without protest, but she didn't seem to be aware of it, any more than she was aware of anything else that was going on. He set the tent up and gently urged her inside, and she obeyed without argument. He made sure that the animals were secure for the night before he crawled into the low tent.

Sara sat just where he'd left her. She hadn't even unzipped her jacket. Without a word, he began to undress her, his fingers sure and efficient. It was only after he'd stripped off his own clothes and eased them both beneath the top sleeping bag that she seemed to become aware of anything.

"Cody?"

"It's all right. Just go to sleep."

She turned in his arms, her fingers running lightly over his chest. He felt a stir of desire, which he firmly suppressed. He felt more than a stir, however, when her fingers slid down his body to gently close around him.

"Sara." Her name came out on a groan and he reached for her hand, intent on drawing her away, but her fingers tightened, starting a soft motion that drew a gasp from him. His hand abandoned her wrist and slid up her back, his fingers sinking into the tangle of her hair. He drew her head back, trying to read her expression in the darkness. All he could see was the glimmer of her eyes and the quick motion of her tongue as she licked her lips.

"Make love to me, Cody. Please? Please, make love to me."

His chest ached at the need in her voice. He wished that he could read her expression. He wished that the blood wasn't pounding so loudly in his temples. It made it difficult to think of anything but the slender length of her against him, beneath him.

Their lovemaking was both tender and passionate, a slow burning flame that exploded in a shower of embers, leaving them both satiated. It was an affirmation of their own lives in the face of the death they'd found. And afterward, Sara cried herself to sleep against his shoulder.

Cody held her, running his hand over her trembling back, soothing her as he would a frightened, exhausted animal. The tears were a safety valve. Nature's way of releasing tension. When she at last lay quiet against him, he continued to hold her, staring into the darkness as if he could see beyond the tent's walls to the future.

His emotions were so tangled around this woman. Such a tiny frame to hold so much power. He shut his eyes, refusing to examine his feelings more closely. He wasn't at all sure he was ready for what he might find.

THE THREE DAYS that followed were surely the longest Sara had ever known. Every day, they started at dawn and rode until darkness hid the trail. She wavered between a giddy feeling of euphoria—Cullen had made it through the crash—and a feeling that this was all some surreal nightmare, and at any moment she would wake up to find none of it had happened. When she felt that way, she had only to look at Cody to know that it was real.

In her more aware moments, she was appreciative of Cody's unending support, the subtle ways in which he tried to reassure her. When she resented stopping for meals, he stayed calm and reasonable, never telling her that she was behaving like an idiot.

Cody's appreciation of Sara's strength rose with each passing day. If it was a strain for him, he knew it was ten times the strain for her. He could feel her tension as if it were his own.

Cullen had left plenty of signs of his passing, and Cody's respect for the boy rose. It was clear that he knew what he was doing. His camps were well planned and carefully arranged. When they at last came upon his footprints in the snow, Sara was ecstatic. It meant that they were not far behind him. And on horseback they could travel at a much faster pace than he could ever hope to make.

Cody was pleased with the footprints also, but they added new worries as well as held out new hope. The pattern was not even. The boy was all but dragging one leg, and once or twice, Cody found signs that Cullen had fallen and that it had been quite a struggle for him to get up again. And overlaying the footprints was the broad, clear track of a coyote.

Dog bristled angrily as he sniffed the coyote's track, and Cody laid his hand on the big dog's neck. "It's probably just a coincidence, boy. Coyotes generally won't mess with a man." Dog growled low in his throat, indicating his opinion of this theory as clearly as if he could speak, and Cody almost smiled as he rose to his feet.

He stared at the footprints fading into the distance. Behind him, Sara sat on her horse with barely concealed impatience. They were so close now. Any delay was all but unbearable. He ignored her for the moment, turning his attention up to the sky. The storm had held off so far, but that good luck couldn't last long.

He stepped into the stirrup and swung back up onto Dancer's back before meeting Sara's impatient look. Today her eyes reflected the bright blue of her coat, like shallow pools on a hot summer day. He wanted to lose himself in the depths of them.

"How far?" Sara's question snapped him out of his preoccupation and he shrugged.

"I can't say exactly, but we're pretty close."

"Will we catch up with him tonight?"

"I don't know."

"But it's possible?"

"It's possible."

"I don't want to stop for lunch. We can eat some jerky while we ride. I want to see Cullen." Her words started out as a firm demand and ended as almost a plea.

Cody hesitated for a moment, his eyes going from her to the heavy clouds and down to the trail. Those coyote prints bothered him. There was something very deliberate about their placement. He nodded. A sense of urgency was tugging at him and he didn't think it was rubbing off from Sara.

"Okay. I won't risk traveling after dark, but we can keep up until then."

A quick word sent Dog ranging ahead of them, his nose sniffing out signs that human senses would miss. The ground was too slippery for the horses to safely do anything faster than a quick walk, and the pace seemed unbearably slow to both Sara and Cody.

At noon they stopped just long enough to dig some jerky out of their packs and give each horse a few handsful of oats. Dog returned, but he hovered on the outskirts of the group, as if impatient with the delay.

By late afternoon it was clear that the tracks they were following were very fresh. It was also clear that darkness was coming on faster than they were gaining on their quarry. Despite his own sense of urgency, Cody was not going to risk taking a fall by traveling after dark. When he could just barely see his hand in front of his face, he drew Dancer to a halt. He could feel Sara's resistance to the move, but Satin stopped next to the stallion.

"We can't risk traveling without light." His voice was kind, but there was no arguing with it.

Sara stared ahead before dragging her eyes back to him. He didn't have to be able to see her expression to read her disappointment. "Couldn't we—"

"Sara, we're not going to do Cullen any good if we get ourselves killed by walking over a cliff in the dark. We'll start again first thing in—" He broke off, his head spinning around. A frisson went up his spine, and it was followed a moment later by a wailing howl that brought the hackles up on both their necks.

"That's Dog." He nudged Dancer to a walk. "He's either in trouble or..."

"Or—" Sara urged Satin after the other horse "—or what?"

"Or he's found Cullen."

The Survivor

THE COYOTE HAD GROWN TIRED of waiting. Cullen could read it in his eyes, in the way he'd grown ever more bold. Cullen's fingers tightened on the grip of the .45 he'd brought with him. Across the fire, he could see the coyote, just a shadow among the darker shadows of the night, too vague to fire at.

Cullen wished he'd brought one of the rifles, but when he'd left the crash, it had seemed as if a rifle would be an unnecessary weight and he'd opted to take only the pistol. With the rifle, he could have put an end to this cat-and-mouse game days ago. But now it was almost as if the coyote knew just how close he could get without risking an air-conditioned hide. He seemed to know that his adversary couldn't get a clear sight of him in the almost-dark night.

Cullen rested the pistol on his good leg, wishing that he could get to his feet. He'd feel better on his feet, but his leg had barely held out long enough for him to gather firewood. There was no way he could stand up all night. He closed his eyes for an instant and then forced them open again. Tonight, he didn't dare sleep.

He rummaged through his pack, coming up with a package of granola bars. They were rather the worse for wear, but he ate one with all the relish he might have shown a sirloin steak at another time and place. He'd only been able to catch one other rabbit since his first success at hunting, and his supplies were getting more than a bit thin.

His hunger was forgotten as the coyote stepped into the edge of the firelight. Cullen felt every muscle in his body tighten as he stared into those golden eyes. For an instant, he was almost hypnotized by their gleaming

depths, and he suddenly understood a rabbit's fasci-
nation with a diamondback. The coyote's upper lip
drew back, displaying a terrifying length of fang, and
Cullen slowly raised the pistol. If he could hit the animal right in the head, the impact of the slug would stop
the coyote before those fangs could reach his throat.

If he missed . . . He gave a mental shrug and refused
to consider that possibility. He was a good shot. And
he had quite an incentive to be accurate. He pulled
back the hammer and his finger curled around the
trigger. Just another second.

Suddenly another shape launched itself out of the
darkness. Cullen threw his arm up in a reflexive action, protecting his throat, but he was not the target.
The coyote was. Cullen had only a brief glimpse of a
massive shape and a muzzle drawn back in an enraged
snarl, and then the two animals disappeared from the
firelight in a mass of rolling fur and teeth. He could
hear their guttural growls and see their movements, but
they were well outside the range of the fire's light.

Bracing himself on the rock wall behind him, he
dragged himself to his feet. The battle sounds ceased
suddenly, and he heard a scuttling noise as the defeated combatant conceded the fight and ran. There
was a moment of silence, and then Cullen heard a
sound that sent ice water through his veins. It was a
howl that echoed in the quiet night, a long ululating
wail that announced death on four feet.

Wolf. Cullen tightened his hold on the revolver. It
wasn't possible. Bounty hunters had long ago cleared
wolves out of this area. But the shadowy form that
stepped into the firelight was too big to be a coyote.
Cullen's finger contracted a little tighter on the trigger, but he didn't pull it. Man and animal faced each

other across the firelight for a long moment before the animal calmly sat down, licking traces of blood from his muzzle. His golden eyes stared at Cullen unblinkingly, but he made no move to come any closer.

Cullen relaxed slowly, taking in the animal's unwolflike markings. A wolf mix, maybe. But just because he appeared to be part dog didn't mean he wasn't a danger. Feral dogs could kill just as efficiently as their wholly wild cousins. This animal had driven off the coyote, but that didn't mean he didn't see Cullen as a meal.

It seemed as if the two stared at each other for hours, but it could only have been a matter of minutes before Cullen heard the unmistakable sound of someone or something large approaching. Hardly daring to hope that it might be what it sounded like—he'd been hoping for too long—Cullen stepped forward, keeping the fire between himself and the wolf dog. The animal was staring into the darkness, and it was obvious that he was familiar with whatever was out there.

The first horse to come into sight was a beautiful bay quarter horse, but Cullen barely noticed its rider, looping the reins around the saddle horn and stepping out of the saddle. Cullen's attention was all for the exquisite little palomino that followed, or more exactly for the palomino's rider.

"Sara." His voice cracked, rusty with lack of use. She slid out of the saddle and ran toward him, and Cullen forgot all about his injured leg as he took a quick step toward her. His knee buckled and he would have gone sprawling, but there was suddenly a solid shoulder beneath his arm and an arm around his waist, bracing him. He was hardly aware of the support.

His arms closed around Sara, hugging her with rib-cracking strength, as he buried his face in her hair. He'd always known she wouldn't rest until she found him. Holding her close, he realized that he was going to make it. He wasn't alone anymore.

Chapter Eleven

It was some time before Sara became aware of anything beyond the fact that Cullen was alive and with her again. Her fingers stayed wrapped around his, as if she feared that loosing her hold on him would result in his disappearance. Her chest hurt with the conflicting urges to laugh, to shout and to cry. The tears that streaked her face provided a needed release for all the emotions that tumbled inside. Cullen's eyes were equally bright, and Sara knew he shared the same confusing mix of emotions.

Cody saw the two of them settled beside the fire and then proceeded to set up camp and feed the horses. It wasn't until he came over to the fire and sat back on his heels across from Sara and the boy that Sara seemed to remember his presence.

"Oh." Her eyes widened with guilt as she realized that she hadn't even introduced the two men. "Cullen, this is Cody Wolf. He's the one who found you. Cody, this is my nephew, Cullen."

"Dr. Livingstone, I presume," Cody murmured as he shook hands with Cullen.

Cullen smiled. "Thank you doesn't seem quite adequate somehow. I'd offer you a seat but I've had all the furniture sent to the cleaners."

"Don't worry about it." Cullen's gutsiness reminded Cody of Sara, and his smile warmed. "How bad is the leg?"

"The leg?" Only then did Sara remember the way Cullen had dragged his leg when he'd come to meet her. "What's wrong with your leg?"

"The knee is pretty busted up."

"Mind if I take a look?"

Cullen measured the other man for a long moment. What he saw was lean features, shadowed by a ragged beard, and eyes that glittered green in the firelight. He nodded.

"Be my guest. But it doesn't look too pretty."

"I suspect I've seen worse." Cody came around the fire and knelt beside Cullen, deliberately placing himself between Sara and the injured leg. "Sara, why don't you heat up some soup? He looks like he hasn't eaten a decent meal in weeks."

Sara's mouth set mutinously. She knew exactly what Cody was trying to do. But before she could say anything, Cullen spoke up.

"I could probably eat a small bear and come up hungry," he said.

Her protest died unspoken. There was no doubting Cullen's sincerity.

While she prepared soup and opened a can of meat, Cody eased apart the leg of Cullen's pants. Cullen had split it along the seam and tied it together with a crude thong. Cody's breath hissed out when he saw the swollen purple mass that bore little resemblance to a joint. His eyes swept up, wondering if the boy realized how bad the injury was. Their eyes met, and Cody saw acknowledgment and acceptance. Without a word, he tied the pants leg together again and stood up.

"How bad is it?" Sara handed Cullen a mug of soup, her eyes seeking Cody's. He shrugged.

"It's way beyond my skills. They should be able to patch it up in a hospital."

"I'm lucky to be alive." Cullen's matter-of-fact tone made it impossible to offer any sympathy on the damage to his leg.

"We didn't have a way to bring Bill with us, so we left him where he was." Sara brought the words out hesitantly.

Cullen stopped eating, his face tightening in a way that made Sara's heart ache. "It's a good place for him. The only thing he loved more than the wilderness was flying."

"It must have been pretty terrible." The words seemed hopelessly inadequate.

"His chest was crushed and he had a fractured skull. He never regained consciousness." Cullen shrugged. "God knows why I'm still alive."

Sara bit her lip, searching for something to ease his pain. But Cullen was not yet ready for sympathy. He picked up his cup, making it clear that the subject was closed.

He drank the soup hungrily, feeling its warmth sink in and fill the hollow in his stomach. He ate the meat more slowly, savoring its flavor.

"Is that your dog?" He nodded his head to where Dog sat.

Cody shrugged. "We keep company. It's a little hard to say that Dog belongs to anyone."

"You might want to check him for wounds. He tangled with a coyote that's been trailing me for a few days."

By the time Dog had been carefully examined and treated for minor scratches, Cullen was beginning to show signs of giving in to exhaustion. Cody glanced up from Dog in time to see Cullen drag his eyelids upward with a visible effort.

"I think it's about time we turned in. You and Sara can take the tent."

Cullen was too exhausted to argue, and a few minutes later he was sleeping heavily, rolled in his sleeping bag. Sara lingered outside, watching Cody feed the fire and clear a space for his sleeping bag.

"Won't you be too cold? We could make room for all three of us in there."

He stepped around the fire to stand beside her, cupping his palm around her cheek. "Without you sharing my bed, I'll be cold no matter where I sleep."

She leaned against him, wrapping her arms around his waist. "I can hardly believe that he's really okay. If it wasn't for you—"

"If it wasn't for a lot of things," he said, cutting her off. He didn't want her gratitude. His fingers slid to the nape of her neck, tilting her head back to receive a slow, arousing kiss. When he released her, Sara gave a breathless little laugh.

"If you wanted to make sure I'd forget to say thank you, you almost succeeded." She raised up on her toes to brush a quick kiss across his mouth. "Thank you, Cody."

She disappeared into the tent, but Cody didn't move for a long moment, staring after her with an arrested look in his eyes. He didn't want her gratitude. The only thing he wanted from her was . . . her love.

He spun on his heel and strode over to his sleeping bag, but he couldn't walk away from the realization that he was in love with Sara Grant. Not the heady, reach-for-the-moon kind of love he'd known once or twice when he was a boy, but a deep, searing emotion that had sunk slowly into his heart and mind. He cursed under his breath as he tugged his boots off.

Crawling into the sleeping bag fully dressed, he tried to shut out the thought. It was late. They had to make an early start tomorrow. It had been a very emotional few days. First finding the crash, and then trailing the boy. He was overly tired. That's all it was. He was just overly tired.

He reached out and fed a few pieces of wood into the fire. Closing his eyes, he made a concentrated effort to fall asleep, but—as vividly as they'd ever been in his dreams—he saw Sara's eyes. A clear violet when she was happy, stormy gray when she was upset or aroused. He shifted restlessly, trying to shut out the image, but his mind refused to let go.

He spent a restless night, waking periodically to feed the fire, his dreams haunted with images of Sara in all her moods. Not the kind of dreams that had drawn him into the mountains. Those had stopped with the finding of the crash site. These dreams reflected only the turmoil in his own mind. At some point, Dog moved to lie down along his side, stretching his bulk out on the edge of the sleeping bag. His presence seemed to offer not only a physical barrier against the cold but a buffer to the ragged circle of Cody's thoughts. Cody at last fell into a deep, dreamless sleep, waking two hours later as the sky lightened from black to purple to sullen gray.

He rolled awake, his mood as gray as the storm clouds. He jammed his feet into his boots and coaxed the smoldering coals back to life. The temperature had dropped since the day before, and he was grateful for the sheepskin lining of his jacket. But nothing could warm the ice that was settling in around his heart. Falling in love with Sara Grant was quite possibly the stupidest thing he'd ever done.

They were night and day. She lived in a city of millions and he lived miles from his nearest neighbor. She was all fragile strength and he was rough edges. Now that they'd found her nephew, they had absolutely nothing in common. When they got down out of the mountains, she would go back to Los Angeles and he would continue as he always had, taking care of the ranch and talking to the horses far more than he did to people.

And once she was gone, he'd forget all about her. In a few weeks, she would be nothing but a half-remembered dream. The thought echoed hollowly but he refused to acknowledge that forgetting Sara Grant might not be that easy.

THE TRIP DOWN out of the Rockies was both easier and more difficult than the journey up had been. They knew exactly where they were going and they were able to take a more direct route from where they found Cullen than the one they'd had to use in reaching the wreck.

Cody spent some time redistributing the packs to give Cullen a horse to ride and then they spent even more time rigging up a support for his injured leg. At first, Sara found herself hovering over her nephew, hardly able to believe that he was really there. After a while she adjusted to the reality of his presence and she began to notice other things.

Like the fact that Cody seemed to be avoiding her. It was so subtle that at first she thought it might be her imagination. The withdrawal was more mental than physical. He didn't get up and move if she sat down next to him. He answered when she spoke, but given a choice he sat on the opposite side of the fire from her, and he never addressed her first if he could avoid it.

It was just because they were no longer alone, she told herself two days after they had found Cullen. Things had changed but it wasn't clear just how they'd changed. Maybe he thought she wouldn't want Cullen to know they had been lovers. And she wasn't sure herself on that point. Cullen was fond of David, though the two of them had absolutely nothing in common except Sara herself. She didn't want Cullen to think that she'd thrown David over on a whim, but she wasn't ashamed of what had happened with Cody, either.

But then, she supposed it really didn't matter that she was uncertain about how to handle the situation, because Cody had apparently made the decision for her. She almost doubted her own memory. Could this polite-but-distant stranger be the same man who had made love to her, teaching her things about herself she'd never known? He'd taught her not only passion, but also how to reach deep inside to find her own strength. He'd taught her that she could survive anything and come out on top.

She glared at Cody's back, frustrated by the way her thoughts went around and around without ever settling on an answer. She couldn't come up with an answer on her own, and getting Cody to talk to her was about as simple as catching a greased pig.

They could even have talked as they rode, but he used Cullen as a shield. If the trail was wide enough to ride three abreast, he placed Cullen in the middle, and if it narrowed down to where they had to ride two abreast, Cody either rode ahead and left her with her nephew or he and Cullen rode together. The problem was that he was much better at maneuvering than she was.

Right now, he and Cullen were at the front of their small caravan. The lone packhorse trailed behind them, leaving Sara to bring up the rear. She huddled deeper into her heavy coat, glaring at the drifting pattern of snowflakes in front of her. It had been snowing since morning. The threatening storm had finally descended, not with a clap of thunder or bolts of lightning, but with a whisper of white flakes.

The snowfall was deceptively gentle. From the looks of the clouds, it wasn't planning on stopping anytime soon, which meant it wouldn't be long before the paths out of the mountains became blocked with snow. She had seen the worry in Cody's eyes when the snow began to fall, but he hadn't said anything.

In fact, he hadn't said anything to her in ages, but he seemed to have plenty to say to Cullen. Her lower lip thrust out in an unconscious pout as she stared at the two males. She was ashamed to admit it, but she couldn't deny a niggling feeling of jealousy. The rapport between the two of them had been so instantaneous and complete that it seemed to shut her out. She should be grateful that they liked each other. She was grateful.

Cullen was a vital part of her life and it was important that he like Cody because Cody was... What? Was he going to be anything at all in her life once they returned to civilization?

Sara's irritation might have been eased if she'd been able to hear the conversation between the two men.

"I really appreciate what you've done for me." Cullen gritted his teeth as his leg was jostled by the rough trail. "I was beginning to wonder if I was going to make it."

Cody glanced at him, noting the lines of pain beside the boy's mouth, but helpless to do anything about them. "I have a feeling you just might have made it without help. You're a lot like your aunt. Stubborn as a mule and you don't give up."

"I see you've run into the core of steel that runs beneath Sara's fragile exterior."

Cody smiled at the apt description. "That just about describes her."

"She's had to be stubborn. When my parents died, she fought the state tooth and nail to get custody of me. They thought she was too young to take care of a twelve-year-old boy. I suppose she was too young. She gave up a lot."

"I don't think she's ever regretted it." Cody leaned forward to brush snow off Dancer's neck.

"No, I suppose she hasn't. She's got a strong sense of responsibility." Cullen reached up to brush the snow off the brim of his hat.

All around them the world was white, deceptively beautiful. The autumn grass was covered with a fresh blanket of snow, still thin enough to be brushed aside to allow the horses to graze, but growing ever deeper, a promise of things to come.

"She gave up her career for me."

Cody turned to look at him, one brow rising in silent question. "I thought she was a model."

"She is, but that's not what she started out to be. She was an art major in college and her professors thought she had a very bright future as a sculptress. She'd done a little hand modeling to pick up some extra cash, but she had to have a solid income before the state would give her permanent custody of me. She worked like a slave until she could show them some contracts and prove that she could make a good living as a model."

"What about her art? Has she kept up with that?"

Cullen shrugged. "Sculpting is hard on the hands. She wouldn't get very many jobs if her nails were short and she had calluses from the tools. I've tried to persuade her to pick it up again, but she won't. I think maybe it hurts too much to work at it part-time. Sara tends to be an all-or-nothing kind of person. She can't do things by half measures."

"No, I don't suppose she can." Cody didn't have to turn to look at her to picture that stubborn chin. With shame he remembered the times he'd watched her soothe lotion into her hands and had chalked it up to vanity. He'd never really stopped to consider that her hands were her source of income, just as his horses were his.

His chest hurt with the pain of her lost dreams. He wanted her to have everything she'd ever wanted. He wanted to be able to give her everything. His mouth twisted bitterly. He wasn't in a position to give her anything. Everything he had was tied up in the ranch, and it would be years before he could take more than a living wage out of the profits.

He pulled the brim of his hat lower over his eyes. It wasn't his problem. Sara meant nothing to him. He admired her courage and her determination, but admiration was all it was. He couldn't let it be more.

Cullen glanced at his companion's profile, wondering what was going on behind those impassive features. It was impossible to read Cody's thoughts, but Cullen could take an educated guess. Several times, he'd caught Cody watching Sara with a look in his eyes that could only be described as hungry. But only when she wasn't looking at him. If she happened to glance his way, he would immediately turn away, concealing his expression from her.

Interesting, Cullen thought. Maybe Sara had found what everyone hoped to find. Someone she could spend her life with. David Turner was a good man and Cullen liked him, but he'd always known that the photographer didn't stir Sara's soul the way a life companion should. Cullen had been only twelve when his parents died, but he could remember the way they'd looked at each other—as if there were no one else in the world. That was what he wanted for himself, and he wanted no less for Sara.

But Cullen's positive thinking was not shared by either Cody or Sara. On the journey out of the mountains, they were together yet apart. The sexual awareness that had been between them from the start was now magnified by the fact that they had been lovers.

Sara had only to look at Cody to remember the rasp of his beard against her breast, the feel of his taut muscles beneath her hands. But she missed the easy companionship that had developed between them even more than having him beside her at night. It had been the two of them against nature, against time, against all odds. And they'd won. They'd beat the odds. Cullen had beat the odds. But somehow, in the winning, Sara had lost Cody. He'd pulled away from her, withdrawing the warmth that had slowly grown between them. Sara missed that warmth. Only now that it was gone had she come to realize just how important it had been to her.

The snow continued to sift down without showing any signs of stopping. It was hard to imagine a time when the world hadn't been covered with a soft white blanket. As the snow deepened, the footing for the horses became more uncertain, and they were forced to slow their pace, a delay that none of them welcomed.

At night, Sara turned over in her sleeping bag, careful not to disturb Cullen, who slept such a short distance away. She stared at the blank wall of the tent. A few feet beyond that thin barrier, Cody lay wrapped in his sleeping bag, sheltered under the same rock overhang that sheltered the tents. He'd refused to share the tent with them, saying that he would be just fine outside with the fire, but Sara had the feeling that he didn't want to be too close to her, as if her nearness could undermine some resolve he'd made.

It hurt to have him push her away. It hurt more than she liked to admit, because if she faced how much it hurt she had to face the depth of her feelings for him, and that frightened her. How had she come to care so much for a man who held his emotions inside?

What was going to happen to them once they returned to civilization? Them? She closed her eyes, trying to shut out the word. She was thinking as if they were a couple, as if there had been some kind of commitment between them, something to pin a future on.

Did she want a future with Cody Wolf? She shifted restlessly, trying to ignore the question. She didn't know what she wanted. How could she want a future with him? How could she bear to walk away?

Outside, Cody reached out to feed the fire, pulling his hand back into the warmth of the sleeping bag as quickly as possible. He'd given up trying to sleep. It wasn't the cold, though his breath created clouds of vapor with his every exhalation. It wasn't a physical discomfort that kept him awake—unless you counted the ache that settled in the pit of his stomach, growing heavier with every step that took him closer to home. Closer to saying goodbye.

He shut his eyes, willing away the image of Sara's walking out of his life, willing away the pain that went with it. He didn't want to feel pain. He didn't want to acknowledge that it might bother him to say goodbye. There was no future in the feelings that he had for her. There could be nothing ahead for the two of them.

She would go back to Los Angeles and pick up the threads of her life and he would stay just where he was, raising horses and struggling to make ends meet. Before long, this whole period of time would seem like a far-off dream, half-remembered and unimportant.

There could be no future with her. No future at all.

Chapter Twelve

The nearer they got to home, the harder it was to remember what they'd gone through. As civilization neared, the days spent in the mountains began to take on a dreamlike quality.

When Sara recognized the pool where she'd bathed and Cody had watched her, she felt like crying. The edges of the pool were now covered by a thin layer of ice, though the stream still ran freely through its center. She looked away, blinking back tears, and her eyes met Cody's. For just a moment she thought she saw a reflection of her own pain in his gaze, and her heart swelled with some emotion she was afraid to identify. But then he looked away, his expression impassive.

The first part of their return trip had taken them over new country. There had been no sense in returning to the crash site to retrace their steps from there. But eventually they ended up on the same path that had led Sara and Cody into the Rockies.

Each familiar landmark brought a squeezing pain to Sara's chest. It was like parting from an old friend every time she thought about never seeing any of this again. Every time she thought about never seeing Cody again.

If Cody felt the same, he concealed it perfectly. It was impossible to read anything of what he was thinking or feeling. He might not have been aware that they'd traveled this way before. Did he remember watching her at the pool, all the arguing they had done, the first time they'd kissed? Was she crazy to remember it all so vividly?

The closer they got to the ranch, the more conflicting were the feelings surging through Sara. It would be wonderful to be back amid such luxuries as running water and real beds. And it would be good to be able to get Cullen to a doctor. Her eyes settled worriedly on her nephew. Though he'd made no complaint, she knew he was in pain. She could see it in the lines that bracketed his mouth, lines that hadn't been there before the crash. He'd grown up far too quickly since then. No boy of eighteen should have a face that reflected that amount of hard-won maturity.

Yes, she'd be glad to return to civilization for many reasons. But when she looked at Cody there was a part of her that longed to turn Satin's head around and retreat back into the mountains, to run away from the parting that lay ahead.

Cody rode a few yards in front of his two companions. The sole packhorse, its burden considerably lighter than it had been when he and Sara began this trip, followed him. Then Cullen and then Sara. There was no particular reason for the way they were strung out along the trail. Perhaps it was just the weariness that was creeping over all of them, the tensions that went with being almost home but not quite there yet. Whatever it was, none of them seemed to have much to talk about.

They would probably make it back to the ranch by nightfall. Cody had announced that much at breakfast this morning. If Sara had conflicting feelings about that piece of information, the horses had no such problem. Sensing that they were nearing home and a nice warm barn, their pace picked up, and Sara found herself having to control Satin, making sure that the mare didn't hurry and risk a fall on the snowy ground.

It was twilight when they at last reached the mouth of the valley. Below them, Cody's ranch spread out in a blanket of gleaming white. In the distance, lights twinkled from the ranch house. By mutual consent they drew their horses to a halt. No one spoke as they stared down at the Western postcard laid out below them.

Sara reached out and took Cullen's hand. The strength of his grip told her that she wasn't the only one who was moved by the moment. She glanced across Cullen at Cody, but it was impossible to read anything in his face, shielded as it was by the double cloak of dim light and the brim of his hat. But Dancer stirred restlessly beneath him, reflecting his rider's emotional turmoil.

Without a word, Cody nudged the stallion forward. The other horses followed suit, and they started the descent into the valley. It was not an easy trip to make on the snowy slope and in the dark. Dog loped ahead, but for the horses it was not such a simple matter. The snow made a treacherous stairway, and more than once they skidded on their rumps, giving their riders a more exciting ride than any of them desired. The darkness didn't make things any easier, but no one suggested camping for the night and making the final leg of the journey in the morning. They were too close to tolerate a delay now.

Reaching level ground, they were forced to keep their pace slow in deference to the lack of light. Traveling the short distance to the ranch house took twice as long as it would have in daylight, but when they at last walked the horses into the ranch yard, it was worth every slow step.

Dog had alerted Billy Williams to their return and he was waiting for them, light spilling out of the barn. Bundled in a heavy coat, he looked twice as big as the gangling youth Sara remembered. She bit her lip fiercely to hold back tears as Satin came to a halt in front of the barn. Now that they were back at last, she was suddenly so tired that she couldn't imagine how her legs would support her once she slid out of the saddle.

"Cody! I was just about to leave for the night when Dog showed up." Billy's young voice cracked with excitement as Cody swung down off Dancer and reached out to clasp the boy's hand. Billy shook Cody's hand but his eyes were on the other two riders. Two. One more than had started out.

"You found the crash! I told Dad you would."

"Billy, this is Cullen Grant." Cody leaned against Dancer for a moment, the first time Sara had seen him show any sign of the exhaustion that must be coursing through him. "How's everything?"

"Just fine. I been takin' care of things for you, just like you asked."

Cody nodded and then forced himself to stand away from the stallion's support. "The horses are beat, and I think we could all use a hot shower and a decent bed."

"I'll stay around and help." It was obvious that the boy would have been heartbroken if Cody had suggested that he go home. Luckily, Cody made no such suggestion. He accepted Billy's help with a quiet thanks that made the boy's chest swell with pride.

Billy helped Cullen ease down off his horse, trying to jar Cullen's injured leg as little as possible. Looking at the two of them in the light that spilled out of the barn, Sara's heart twisted with pain. There couldn't be more than a year or two between them, but where Billy's face had the open, wide-eyed wonder of youth, Cullen's face was tight with pain and maturity. He'd grown up these past few weeks and there was nothing Sara could do to give him back his youth.

"Don't worry too much. He'll be okay." When Cody spoke she tore her eyes away from the two boys and looked down at him. For once, she could read his expression. The vibrant green of his eyes were soft with understanding, and she had to blink back tears.

"He's aged so much."

"He's been through a lot. Now, do you plan on staying on that horse all night or would you like me to give you a hand down?" It was the longest sentence he'd addressed to her in days, and Sara found herself smiling at him.

"I was thinking about just staying up here. It seems much easier." She bent to rest her hands on his shoulders and he swung her off the horse with easy strength. He didn't release her even when her feet hit the ground, and Sara tilted her head back to look up at him. From this angle, the brim of his hat once again shadowed his eyes, but she could feel his searching look.

Sexual tension flared to life between them. They had barely touched in the days since they'd found Cullen, but their awareness of each other hadn't died. It had only been banked down, waiting for something to fan it to life. They stared at each other in silence. His hands tightened on her rib cage, and Sara's hands slid toward the back of his neck. His head seemed to dip and she stopped breathing, her mouth softening in anticipation of his kiss.

The door of the house slammed and Billy clattered down the steps, his boots making enough noise to wake the dead. Cody dropped his hands as if burned, and Sara stepped back, her eyes not meeting Cody's.

"I got Cullen settled. He says he hopes you don't mind him using the shower."

"Sure." Cody tugged his hat lower and turned to gather up Satin's reins. "You might as well go on up to the house, Sara. Billy and I will take care of the horses. There's a shower in the barn that I'll use, so you might as well clean up at the house."

He turned away without waiting for an answer. Billy gave her a shy grin. "It must feel great to be back."

Sara dragged her eyes away from Cody's back and managed a faint smile. "Just great."

REALLY TERRIFIC. If she just kept telling herself that, maybe she'd be able to believe it. She rolled over in bed and stared at the ceiling. It would be dawn soon. And when Cullen woke, they would get in her car and drive away from this little valley, leaving Cody to get on with his life. And she would get on with hers. Heaven knows, she didn't want to stay here. Did she?

Why couldn't she go back to sleep? She'd slept like a log until half an hour ago, when she'd come awake with a suddenness that made her heart pound. The house was quiet. She'd adjusted to the silence during the time they'd spent in the mountains. It had begun to seem normal not to hear traffic noise and sirens. But, back within four walls, the silence seemed strange. Unnatural.

Across the hall, Cullen was presumably still asleep. As she would be if she had any sense. He'd taken Cody's room, too tired to make even a token protest when Cody said he'd sleep on the couch. She'd helped Cullen to bed after his shower, and he'd been asleep before she shut the door behind her.

She'd been almost as tired. So, what was she doing awake before dawn? She curled up on her side and stared at the dark wall. Why wasn't she asleep? Because all she could think of was Cody. And saying goodbye to him. She didn't want him to ask her to stay, did she?

Yes. The answer came straight from her heart, surprising her with its intensity. More than she'd ever wanted anything in her life, she wanted him to ask her to stay with him. Not just as a sexual partner, but as a life companion. She swallowed a lump in her throat. She'd fallen in love with him. She'd been running away from that knowledge for days now, refusing to admit her feelings, even to herself.

It was just that they'd been through a tremendous amount together. There was desperation in the thought. That's all it was. They'd been thrown into one another's company under emotionally charged circumstances, and a perfectly natural sexual attraction had combined with those circumstances to make her think she was in love with him.

But the knowledge refused to be suppressed. Whether she liked it or not, she was in love with Cody Wolf. In love as she'd never been in her life. But there could be no future for them. Her life was in Los Angeles. His lay in these mountains.

Did he love her? The question was one that people in love had asked through the centuries, but its urgency was not diluted by age. Staring wide-eyed into the darkness, Sara went over every moment of their time together, searching for some clue to his feelings. He wanted her. She didn't doubt that. But did he love her?

Without conscious thought, she shoved back the blankets, shivering as the cool air penetrated her cotton nightshirt. Barefoot, she padded to the door and opened it a crack, peering into the hallway before slipping out. There was a fire going in the fireplace in the living room and the flickering light beckoned her.

She felt almost as if she stood outside her body, watching her feet carry her closer to the flickering light. She stepped around the corner and into the living room and stopped, suddenly aware of what she was doing. Her eyes skipped around the room, avoiding the wide sofa.

The huge painting of the wolf still dominated the room, the eyes gleaming in the firelight as he seemed to watch her. But this time that gaze didn't bother her. The rest of the room was the same—scuffed floors and battered furniture that she remembered, a stack of *National Geographic*s spilling off a corner table, a braided rug adding a touch of warmth to the plain room.

When she could delay it no longer, she at last looked at the figure stretched out on the long sofa. He'd covered himself with only a light blanket, trusting the heat of the fire to keep the chill away. His eyes were closed, and Sara crept forward, hardly daring to breathe. She didn't know what she was doing here. She didn't know what she was going to say if he should wake to find her watching him, but she couldn't turn away. Like a moth to a flame, she was drawn to him.

He'd shaved when he cleaned up, and she realized that she'd forgotten the strength of his jaw, the high curves of his cheekbones. At that moment, with the firelight casting shadows over his lean features, his heritage was plain to read. He looked every inch the warrior.

Her eyes skimmed upward and she froze as they met his. She didn't know how long he'd been watching her, but there was no grogginess in his gaze. He was wide awake and alert. She swallowed hard, trying to think of something to say, some explanation for her presence.

But, in the end, she didn't have to say anything. Staring at him, she found herself mesmerized by the way the firelight caught in his eyes, making them seem to burn with green flames. She took a step nearer, as if compelled. She wanted to warm herself on that flame. He sat up, and the blanket slid to his waist. Sara was aware of the broad strength of his chest, the black hair that curled across the muscles, but she couldn't drag her eyes from his.

She always had been fascinated by fire. When forest fires raced through the mountains near Los Angeles, the flames were sometimes visible from her home, jumping along the ridges of the mountains. She'd watch them, fascinated by the orange light, thinking that it was a tragedy that something so beautiful should be so destructive.

And now she found herself drawn to the green fires in his eyes. A fire that was potentially as destructive to her as any forest fire.

He stood up, the blanket forgotten on the sofa. Thin briefs molded his hips, contrasting with the warm copper of his skin. Sara closed her eyes against the impact of him. This was insanity. She should turn and walk away while there was still time. But there was no more time. His hands touched her shoulders. She could feel the faint rasp of calluses put on his palms by years of hard work.

Her eyes opened languidly to meet the fire of his, her hands coming up to slide around his neck. He bent, his eyes never leaving hers. She waited for his mouth to touch hers, feeling the pounding of her pulse as if it were a drumbeat. Her breath left her in a half sob when his mouth at last found hers. He braced himself, feet apart, catching her slight weight as she sagged against him.

They kissed like lovers separated for years, or like lovers about to part.

Sara's mouth opened to the marauding thrust of his tongue. His hands slid around her back, crushing her to the burning heat of his body, while her hands tightened around his neck as he bent and lifted her into his arms. His lips never leaving hers, he carried her from the firelit warmth of the living room to the cool darkness of her bedroom. Sara didn't feel the change in temperature. She didn't feel anything except Cody. He could have carried her out into the snowy night and she wouldn't have cared. All that mattered was that he was holding her, and that she wanted him to never let her go.

Frantic hands stripped the scraps of fabric from their bodies. The springs creaked as they fell to the bed, arms wrapped around each other. He tasted the delicate skin at the bend of her elbow, the tingling place behind her knee, the shadowy well of her navel.

Sara's hands traced every sweat-sleeked muscle. He felt so right beneath her hands. She arched, her throat taut as his tongue found the very heart of her desire. She twisted, her nails digging into his shoulders as he drove her closer and closer to fulfillment. The pleasure was intense but she wanted him with her. She didn't want to walk this path alone. Her hands tightened, tugging demandingly on his shoulders until, reluctantly, he abandoned the sweet territory he'd conquered.

He slid up her body. Sara opened to him, her thighs cradling his hips, her hands tangling in the darkness of his hair. His mouth closed over hers at the same moment that he claimed her for his own. Sara's whimper of satisfaction was caught in his throat, his moan of completion swallowed by hers. They were joined in a more than physical union. Two halves of one soul locked together.

There was an element of despair in their lovemaking. Each of them wondering if this was the last time. The sweet friction of his body on hers brought tears to Sara's eyes. Tears of love, need and fear. They drew it out, savoring every moment. But the passion was too intense to last forever. Sara felt as if she shattered in a million pieces, all flying outward, and yet she was anchored to earth by the inferno of Cody's body over hers. He stiffened, his body shuddering, and for just an instant, she could believe that he was all hers, that nothing would ever separate them.

It was a long, long time before he gathered the energy to shift off her, rolling to one side in the wide bed but slipping his arm under her neck to draw her close.

Sara closed her eyes, not wanting to see the faint tinge of gray that was creeping in through the window. She didn't want to know that morning had arrived.

"It's going to be light soon." Cody spoke the words she'd been trying not to think, breaking the silence that had lain between them.

"I suppose so." Her fingers combed lightly through the hair on his chest. "I guess Cullen and I will leave as soon as he gets up." *Ask me to stay.*

"I guess so." His hand slid through the warm silk of her hair.

"It's funny, but I'm going to miss this." *I'm going to miss you.*

"After a few days in Los Angeles, it will all seem like a dream." He let his thumb slide along the line of her jaw.

"Maybe. Los Angeles doesn't seem quite so appealing now." *Please ask me to stay.*

"It won't take long to get back into your old life." He fought down the urge to beg her not to go.

"Maybe I don't want my old life." Her mouth shook and she didn't look up at him, afraid to let him see the desperation in her eyes. That was as close as she could come to telling him she wanted to stay.

His hand stroked her shoulder, learning the delicate contours, mapping her collarbone. His eyes looked out over her head, staring at the roughly plastered wall showing worn paint where the rising sun caught it.

"You know, my mother gave up everything when she married my father. Her family were strict Catholics and they were very much of the old country. They never forgave her for marrying outside the faith and marrying an Indian on top of it. They never had any contact with her from the day she walked out of their house to marry my father.

"I asked her once if she didn't miss them, and she said that everyone had to make choices in life. She'd made hers and her family had made theirs, and regrets couldn't change the decisions made.

"She loved my father, but it wasn't an easy life. He tried so desperately to fit into the White Man's world, and he felt he had to deny his heritage to do that. So he did deny it. And the older I got, the more I saw that he'd become little more than a shadow of a man.

"A big reason he made the choices he did was that he wanted to make my mother happy, because he had a deep shame about being Indian and he didn't want that shame to rub off on her. So they bounced from place to place, never really settling anywhere.

"I never doubted that they loved each other, but they were two of the loneliest people I think I've ever known. Each gave up everything to make the other happy, and it left them with little to give."

His hand slid absently up and down her back, but he was looking into the past, touching on old memories. Sara wondered if he even remembered who he was talking to.

"Mother died when I was sixteen and my father died six months later, and I can remember standing at her grave and swearing that I would never love a woman who was so far removed from my life. No one would ever give up everything for me, nor I for her. I would never ask that of anyone."

Sara wondered if it was possible for a heart to physically break. She closed her eyes, squeezing back tears. He couldn't put it much more clearly than that. Even if it had been possible for him to love her, he wasn't going to let it happen. He wasn't going to ask her to stay.

It was for the best, she told herself fiercely. No matter how she felt, their lives lay a thousand miles apart. If he had asked her to stay she might have been foolish enough to agree, but it could never have worked out. Besides, what she felt for him was undoubtedly a product of their being thrown together under extraordinary circumstances.

Once back in L.A., this would all fade back into perspective. She had her job and Cullen, and of course, David was waiting for her. It didn't matter that she couldn't bring David's face to mind. He loved her and their lives lay along similar paths. They could make a good life together.

She shifted with a suddenness that startled a grunt of surprise from him. Her slim body fit neatly over the hard planes of his, her eyes gleaming with some emotion he couldn't read as she looked down at him. It was no longer possible to deny that dawn had arrived. The room was bathed in a clear light that illuminated the two lovers with gentle clarity.

Sara curled her legs along the outside of his hips, her breasts brushing tantalizingly across the furred surface of his chest. His eyes flared with emerald light and his body stirred beneath her. Sara gave him a slow smile, invitation in her eyes.

For just a little while longer, she wanted to pretend that she wouldn't be walking away from him. She wanted to pretend that it was all going to work out as it did in storybooks. She wanted to pretend that he was hers to keep.

Their coming together was explosive, hard, powerful and fast, leaving destruction in its wake. Lying across his body afterward, Sara felt drained, hopeless in a way she'd never known before. She wanted to close her eyes and shut out reality.

Cody savored the feel of her slight weight on top of him. His heart was still pounding, and a damp sheen of perspiration molded them together. Her hair lay like a skein of golden silk across his chest. The last time. He shut out the little voice that tolled the end. If he let himself really absorb the fact that this was the last time, he might not be able to restrain the urge to scoop her up in his arms and lock her away forever.

Pain lanced through him, and his arms tightened across her back. He'd come as close as he could to telling her how he felt. If she chose to walk away, there was nothing he could do to stop her. He'd rather lose her now than get caught in the destructive pattern his parents had followed.

They lay there without speaking, each dreading what the coming day would bring, neither speaking their fears out loud. With each upward movement of the sun they were that much closer to the moment of goodbye. A moment neither of them was sure they had the strength to face.

Sara at last sought refuge in sleep, forcing her mind to empty and letting herself drift away on a sea of forgetfulness. Cody listened to her breathing even out and told himself that he should leave. There were always things to be done on a ranch. Every daylight hour had to be used. But his hands tightened, shifting her into a more comfortable position. Just a little while longer.

This time would have to last him the rest of his life.

Chapter Thirteen

If Sara thought she'd reached the absolute nadir of misery with the realization that there could be no future for her with Cody, she discovered that that had been nothing compared to the pain of walking away.

She'd been alone when she woke, and for a moment she'd wondered if the whole thing had been a dream. But there was a delicate soreness in her muscles that had nothing to do with long hours spent in the saddle. No, she hadn't dreamed any of it.

She began to wonder again when she confronted Cody's totally impassive features over the breakfast table. There was no hint of last night's impassioned lover. They might have been casual acquaintances for all the interest he showed in her. There was far more warmth in his attitude toward Cullen.

And he didn't change. He helped her pack her things into her car, helped Cullen ease his stiff leg onto the floorboards, made sure that she felt confident about driving on the snow-covered roads and then stepped back from the car. Sara pulled her door shut with a distinct slam. If he could be so cool about it, then so could she. She put the car in gear, but her foot hesitated on the gas. For just an instant, her eyes met his through the glass, imprinting this last picture of him on her mind. It had to last her forever.

He was wearing jeans and boots and a sheepskin-lined denim jacket. A battered cowboy hat shaded his face from the white sunlight reflecting off the snow, but she didn't have to be able to see his features. They were imprinted in her mind's eye as firmly as her own were.

Dog sat beside him, as impassive as the man. His yellow eyes gleamed at her, but she couldn't tell whether or not he would be sorry to see her go. The man and dog were appropriate companions. Both of them born for this country. Each walking through life without commitments to another.

With a mental curse she forced herself to turn away, and her foot pressed the accelerator. The reason the landscape was foggy was because the defroster wasn't working very well. It had nothing to do with tears in her eyes.

She felt Cullen's eyes on her, but he didn't say anything until the car rattled across the cattle guard and out under the wooden archway that announced the ranch.

"I think the pair of you are the biggest fools I've ever met." His tone was so conversational that it took her a moment to realize what he'd said. The look she threw him would have melted snow at thirty paces. He was not visibly chastened but he didn't add anything to the one statement.

The snowplows had been at work, and the highways to Denver were clear of snow. Sara almost wished they had been covered with snow. It would have given her something to keep her mind off Cody Wolf.

By the time they got to Stapleton Airport, Sara was so numb that she couldn't even get up the energy to be afraid of flying. She'd asked Billy Williams not to call anyone about Cullen's rescue. She would make all the necessary calls from L.A. Cullen was in no condition to answer endless questions, and she couldn't bear to linger so close to Cody.

She busied herself with seeing to Cullen's comfort, shutting out both the big jet and thoughts of what she'd left behind. Cullen let her fuss, knowing that she needed it more than he did. He assured her for the twentieth time that he wasn't afraid to fly again, pointing out that there was very little connection between an airliner and a small plane. She clutched at his hand anyway, and he let her. She needed the human contact.

The flight was uneventful, and they landed at LAX in the early afternoon. It had been cold and snowy in Denver, but Los Angeles was bathed in smoggy sunshine and the temperature hovered near eighty. The change was hard to adjust to, and Sara found herself trying to shed her warm coat, find her sunglasses and remember where to catch the bus that would take them to her car. But at least she didn't have time to think of Cody.

In fact, she had little time to think about anything or anyone but Cullen over the next few days. They hadn't taken him to a doctor in Denver because he wanted to see a specialist who had once treated his father. Sara had argued at first, but Cullen pointed out, with a pragmatism that was almost frightening, that the damage to his knee had already set as much as it was going to. One day's delay wasn't likely to do any more harm.

She couldn't argue with that, but she did insist on calling the doctor from the airport and driving Cullen right to his office. From there, he was immediately put in the hospital for a battery of tests and a series of X rays to assess the damage to his leg.

Somewhere in between all the visits to the hospital, she found time to call the authorities in Colorado to give them the details of Cullen's rescue and Bill Taylor's death. But Cody had been there ahead of her. When she called John Larkin, she found that he already knew everything he needed to know. He was upset that she hadn't called him before leaving the state, but he couldn't argue with her desire to get Cullen to a doctor as quickly as possible.

He told her how happy he was that she'd found her nephew safe and sound, but there was an underlying tension in his voice that made Sara remember Cody's comment that he was uneasy with things that couldn't be explained in a clear, logical manner. It wasn't that Larkin wished she hadn't found Cullen; he just wished she'd done it in a more conventional manner.

He'd already set the official wheels in motion. They were trying to trace down Bill's next of kin. Sara knew of no one, and if indeed it turned out that he had no family, they would take into advisement Cullen's request that they leave the body where it was. Bill had loved the wilderness, and it seemed a fitting place for him to be laid to rest.

Sara hung up the phone feeling as if a just-healing wound had been opened again. The contact with Cody, however distant, was painful. She wanted to turn around to find him there. She was worried sick about Cullen and she longed for someone to share that worry with. David had been doing a shoot in San Francisco when she returned and wasn't expected back for another two days, but even if he had been there, she couldn't see herself turning to him.

She forced herself to stand up and walk into her bedroom. She had only come home to call Larkin. Now that that duty was taken care of, she wanted to get back to the hospital as soon as possible. One day soon she was going to have to pick up the threads of her life, but not quite yet. All she had the energy for right now was to concentrate on Cullen, on his recovery.

"THE LIMP should be slight, hardly noticeable. You can see how the cartilage will knit here and here." Sara stared at the pictures the doctor was holding up without seeing them. Her hand reached out and found Cullen's, squeezing his fingers without looking at him.

The doctor continued to talk, showing exactly what the damage to the knee had been and just what they were going to do to repair it. He didn't seem aware that he'd lost at least half of his audience.

Sara didn't look at Cullen until after the doctor had finished, closing the door behind him, apparently confident that he'd delivered good news. When she at last turned her eyes to her nephew, he was staring at the wall opposite his hospital bed, his face totally without expression. He looked so much older than his eighteen years that she wanted to weep for the lost youth he could never recover.

"Cullen?"

He blinked and turned his eyes to her. His mouth stretched in a smile but there was little humor in the expression. "It's okay, Sara."

"I'm sorry."

His fingers tightened on hers in acknowledgment. "I know. I was hoping for better news, but I didn't really expect it." He stared at his immobilized leg. "I think I knew that the damage was too bad for them to repair it completely."

"Oh, Cullen, I'm so sorry." She blinked to hold back tears. His words were calm, but she could see the agony in his eyes, could feel it as if it were her own. At his age, to be told that he would limp for the rest of his life was hardly good news. He let his head fall back on the pillows and shut his eyes. The gesture might have shut her out, but the way his fingers tightened on hers told her that he wanted her there.

Hesitantly, she reached up to brush the dark blond hair back from his forehead. She wanted to put her arms around him as she had when he was a boy and tell him that she'd make it all right. But he wasn't a boy anymore and this wasn't something that she could make all right.

"I'm so sorry." She could only repeat the helpless words.

He shrugged. "It could have been a lot worse. I'm lucky to be alive in the first place. A gimpy leg isn't that bad." His voice cracked and his features twisted in angry rejection. "Damn it!"

"It's all right." Sara blinked back her own tears, searching for some way to comfort him.

"No it's not all right! Bill's dead and I'm alive and there's no sense in it. It's not fair!" He turned restlessly, as if trying to pull away from the whole situation. His breath hissed from between clenched teeth as he twisted his injured knee and Sara could see the pain lance through him. Color drained from his face, and he collapsed back onto the bed, his hand tightening painfully on hers.

She reached for the button to call the nurse, but he shook his head, sensing her movement though his eyes were still closed.

"It's all right." Sara hesitated and then let her hand drop away from the button. Cullen was no fool. If he thought he'd done any real damage, he wouldn't try to tough it out.

His eyes opened. Though the pain was still there, she could read the beginnings of acceptance. "The bottom line is that I'm lucky to be alive."

"I wish there was something I could do or say to make this easier. It isn't fair, but there's not much we can do to change things."

"You know, I can remember Dad telling me that life wasn't fair and any fool who thought it was going to be was in for a rude awakening."

"I can remember him telling me the same thing. I...I wish he were here now. I just have the feeling that he'd know what to do or what to say to make you feel better."

Cullen's fingers tightened on hers. "He couldn't do any better job than you have, Sara. You've never let me thank you for always being there. It can't have been easy for you."

"Hush. You're my family, Cullen. I needed you just as much as you needed me. I don't ever want you to feel like I did you a big favor."

"Family. What would we do without them?" His mouth twisted in a half smile, and Sara knew that he would come to terms with the doctor's prognosis. It might not be easy, but Cullen was a survivor.

SHE DROVE HOME, parking the car in the driveway and staring at the little house as if seeing it for the first time.

In the days since their return from Colorado, she'd slept very little. Not only did the walls of her bedroom seem to close in on her, but the bed felt too soft and the usual low hum of traffic seemed to screech in her ears. She'd become accustomed to the silence of the mountains and the city noise seemed intolerable.

With a sigh, she climbed out of the car. She had to stop thinking about Colorado and the mountains and, most of all, Cody Wolf. That was a time that was past and she had to let it go. She let herself into the house, trying not to notice how small it seemed. Throwing her purse on the sofa, she crossed directly to the little desk that sat in one corner of the living room. It was time to cut the last tenuous link between them.

Sitting down at the desk, she pulled out a piece of stationery and drafted a polite little note thanking Cody for finding Cullen and telling him that the prognosis for his leg was good. Reading it over, she decided that it sounded like something that Emily Post might have written to thank someone for a birthday gift. But she refused to change it. It was best to keep things very impersonal. There could be nothing between them, and she didn't want to pretend otherwise. She read the note over one last time and then got out her checkbook and wrote out a check for twenty-five thousand dollars. Her hands was shaking as she added her signature to the bottom.

After sealing the envelope, she had to take a few deep breaths before she could steady her hand enough to address it. Just writing his name sent a surge of pain through her. Before she could change her mind, she snatched up her purse and hurried out of the house. If she didn't mail it now, she might chicken out, and that would only drag things out.

As she watched the envelope disappear into the slot at the post office, she felt as if she had just cut out her heart. That envelope represented her last link with Cody. Once that check was cashed, she would have only memories.

That was good, she told herself firmly. The sooner she broke the connections, the sooner she could get on with her life. She was relieved to have the whole thing over and done with. It was only relief that made her cry herself to sleep that night.

The next morning she dragged herself out of bed and practically crawled into the bathroom to go through the motions of getting ready to face the day. Cullen wasn't expecting her until the afternoon, and the hours between then and now stretched out with appalling emptiness. Her head hurt and her eyes felt as if they were filled with sandpaper. She threw water on her face, trying to rid herself of the gritty feelings.

When she looked in the mirror she was struck by the utter hopelessness in her eyes. Columbine eyes, Cody had called them. But at the moment they looked more like empty holes than mountain flowers. With a disgusted grimace, she tossed her washcloth into the sink and dug through a cabinet searching for a mud pack.

If nothing else, she had to take care of herself so that she could earn a living and afford to pay back David's loan. She had always hated fictional heroines who lay back with die-away airs when they lost their lovers. She was damned if she was going to become one herself. She'd get through this. It might hurt a lot, but she'd make it through.

Two hours later she parked her car behind David's studio and got out. The weather had turned from sunshine to threatened rain with a speed typical of

Southern California. In deference to the gray skies and the hint of dampness in the breeze, she was wearing a pair of light wool trousers and a bulky purple sweater that reflected in her eyes. Her makeup was perfectly applied, her nails were manicured and her expression was serene. If someone looked closely, they might see a look of emptiness in the depths of her eyes, but they'd have to look deep to find it.

Her fingers tightened on the strap of her shoulder bag as she climbed the steps to David's studio and knocked on the door. She wasn't quite sure how to react to him, what to say. She'd left a message with his answering service letting him know that Cullen had been found and telling him that she'd be in touch soon, but she'd deliberately left the impression that the two of them were still in Colorado. She hadn't been quite ready to deal with David. She wasn't sure she was ready now, but she didn't see any reason to put it off.

It was still fairly early in the day, and she knew David was likely to be home. She almost hoped he wouldn't be. That would give her a little more time to decide what she was going to say to him. But the door opened and she was standing face-to-face with a man she had seriously considered marrying only a few short weeks ago.

He looked just the same. Shaggy brown hair and lean features, his tall, lanky body clad in a moth-eaten crewneck sweater and jeans. His brown eyes lit with pleasure when he saw her, and Sara felt like a worm. She cared for David, really cared for him. How was she supposed to look him in the eye and tell him that their relationship could go no farther because she'd slept with a man she'd known only a few days and then compounded the error by falling in love with him?

"Sara!" David swept her off her feet, squeezing her tight and swinging her into his studio before setting her down. He bent and she accepted his kiss, fighting the urge to pull away. When he lifted his head his eyes seemed to search hers for a moment, but he said nothing and she thought perhaps she'd imagined the look.

She stepped away, trying to look casual. "You're not in the middle of a shoot or anything, are you? I probably should have called first."

He shut the door and then leaned against it, his eyes following her as she wandered into the room that served as a living room and sometimes the setting for his photographs. "You never have to call first, Sara. You know that. When did you get back to L.A.?"

"We've been back a few days. I called your service and they said you were in San Francisco or I would have come over sooner."

"I called them every day to see if there'd been any word from you. When they gave me your message, I had the impression that you were still in Denver or I would have called you right away."

"Oh, that's okay. I haven't been home much anyway." She picked up a lens and turned it idly in her hand. The smile she gave him showed her nerves. "I've been spending most of my time at the hospital."

"How is Cullen? You didn't really say anything beyond the fact that he was alive. And his friend?"

He stepped away from the door, and Sara set down the lens and moved farther into the room. "Bill was killed in the crash." She forced another smile, her eyes not quite meeting his. "But Cullen is going to be all right. He tore up his knee and the doctor say's he'll probably always have a slight limp, but he'll walk."

"I'm sorry about his friend." He watched her nervous movements for a moment, feeling a knot settle in his gut. "Want a glass of orange juice? Something nice and healthy to start out the day? Have you eaten yet? I could fix some breakfast."

Sara shook her head. "I'm not really hungry, thanks. But orange juice would be pleasant, if it's no trouble." She didn't really want the juice, but it would give her something to do with her hands. David disappeared into the kitchen, and she took a few deep breaths, forcing herself to sit down. This was David. They'd been friends long before they became lovers.

Her smile was a little more natural when he returned and handed her a glass of juice. She took a sip, hoping he didn't notice her relief when he sat on a chair across from her rather than on the sofa beside her.

"So, it seems you were right all along about Cullen. How did you go about finding him? Was it this guy that the search-and-rescue people suggested?"

Sara looked into her glass, fighting down the surge of pain and gathering her thoughts. She nodded slowly. "He really did know the mountains very well. We traveled on horseback into the mountains and found Cullen and came back out. There's really not much more to say than that."

David knew Sara well. He had caught her every expression on camera. He'd studied her face as both an artist and a lover. He knew when she was lying to him, or at least not telling the whole truth.

"This guy must have been pretty incredible. What was his name?"

The silence stretched out for a moment and then Sara nodded slowly. "Cody Wolf. And he was pretty incredible."

There was something in her quiet words that tightened the knot in his stomach. When he'd watched her drive away, he'd had the feeling that he was watching her go away forever. Since she'd been gone, he'd managed to convince himself that it had been just his imagination working overtime. All she'd done was say another man's name, but there was a note there he'd never heard before. Her tongue caressed the name in a way he'd have sold his soul to hear applied to his own name.

He got up and crossed to the window, staring out. The threatened rain had arrived, and it streamed down across the gray streets of L.A. like a thick wet blanket. The clouds pressed down on the city, seeming to smother all the light out of it. Even the park across the street looked a depressing gray-green.

Behind him, he heard the faint clink as Sarah set her glass down, and he closed his eyes, shutting out the gray scene outside. But there was a grayness in his heart, too. He'd lost her. Just as he'd always known he would. He'd loved Sara Grant ever since she first came to his studio, scared out of her wits, pale with fright but determined to earn a living for herself and her nephew. It had taken him years to slowly cultivate their relationship, coaxing her into friendship, and from there into becoming his lover.

Recently, he'd even begun to think that they might make a good marriage together. He knew he didn't set her soul on fire, but she loved him and they could have a good life. Sara was twenty-eight. If she hadn't found the love of her life by now, maybe she never would. But now that dream was gone. And he had to decide where to go from here.

Rage burned inside him, and he wanted to yell at her to get out of his sight. He turned, not even sure what he was going to say to her. She was looking at him and there was so much pain and regret in her eyes that he felt all the anger drain away.

He'd liked her before he'd loved her. Whatever had happened in Colorado, it hadn't made her happy. With a rueful smile for his own stupidity, he knew that he'd rather have her friendship than nothing at all.

"There's a great assignment coming up for Widmark Jewelers. Could bring in a very tidy sum of money for the lucky pair of hands that wins it. I suggested your name and showed them some of your work, and they seemed very interested. Are you in the market for a job?"

Sara saw the pain in his eyes and she wanted to explain, to offer some apology. But she also read pride and acceptance. Her mouth trembled and she could feel the sting of tears as she nodded.

"I just wrote a check for twenty-five thousand dollars that comes out of your account. It might be a good idea if I found some work so I could pay it back."

"Great. I'll set up an appointment for you tomorrow. Do your nails a pale pink. That will let the jewelry stand out. If they want to go for something darker, they can let us know after they hire you."

"Thank you, David." He knew that she was thanking him for far more than the possibility of a job, but he didn't allow the knowledge to show in his eyes.

"No problem. You're one of the best. It does me good to have your work in my portfolio." He glanced at his watch, pretending he had another appointment, wanting her to go. He needed some time to deal with their changed relationship, time to come to terms with it. Sara immediately stood up.

"I'd better let you get back to work. I'm due at the hospital soon."

She hesitated at the door, her eyes searching his face. He shoved a clenched fist into his pocket and shook his head, his mouth tight.

"Don't."

After a moment that seemed to stretch out forever, she nodded and hurried out of the studio. David shut the door behind her and then leaned back against it, listening to the click of her heels as she walked down the stairs and out of his life. He didn't have another appointment, but there was a limit to just how damned noble he could be.

IT DIDN'T TAKE LONG for life to settle into a pattern. On the surface, everything was much as it had been before Cullen's disastrous camping trip. Within two weeks Cullen was home again. The crutches he had to use even began to seem normal. Sara had already worked on several short assignments. She'd done runway work at a charity showing of petite fashions, plastering a smile on her face and gliding along as if she hadn't a care in the world. Her hands had dialed a telephone to demonstrate just how easy it was to call an advertiser, whose name she couldn't even remember.

It seemed as if life was settling back into old patterns. Of course, some things had irrevocably changed. Cullen was reevaluating his life. David was gradually making the transition from lover to friend, and Sara was grateful for the fact that he cared enough to make the effort.

She should have been pleased with the way things were going. But she was miserable. Instead of fading into the background, the time in Colorado began to seem much more real and vivid than the life she was living now. Every night, Cody walked through her dreams smiling, angry, worried, sensual. His every mood, his every expression penetrated her thoughts. She wondered how winter was treating him. She watched the weather reports for news of the weather in that part of the country.

She had thought the pain would go away after a while, but it seemed to grow every day. She had hoped that, unfed, her love would fade away and die, but love is a flower that sometimes thrives on suffering, and each day she seemed to remember some new thing about him that she loved.

His eyes haunted her until, when she looked in the mirror, she was almost surprised to see her own clear amethyst instead of a vivid emerald green. She wanted to know what was happening on the ranch. She wanted to share in his dreams. It gave her some small consolation to think that the money she had sent him would be put to use making his dreams come true. At least she could feel that she had a part in his dreams, however small.

Christmas came and went, but the holiday spirit was distinctly lacking in her heart. She went through all the motions, but she couldn't help comparing the gray Los Angeles rain to the fresh blanket of snow she'd have in Colorado. Was Cody celebrating Christmas alone?

It wasn't just missing Cody that kept her unhappy. She'd never before regretted her decision to give up sculpting and go into modeling. Modeling had enabled her to take care of Cullen and nothing had been more important than that. She missed her art. Sometimes she missed it so badly that it was like a burning ache inside, but she hadn't regretted the decision. Since returning to California, however, she found herself wandering into art stores and fingering the equipment. Everywhere she looked, she seemed to see something she'd like to try and capture in clay.

Once or twice Cullen brought up the subject of Cody, but Sara refused to discuss him. She didn't want to hear what Cullen had to say. She would get over this. She had responsibilities here that she couldn't just walk away from, even if Cody had wanted her. And he didn't want her. He'd made that clear.

The day after Christmas there was an envelope in the mail from Colorado. There was no return address, only the red postmark, but Sara's hands started to shake. Cody. It had to be from Cody. She forced herself to walk calmly back into the house, oblivious to the fact that she walked through two puddles on the way up the walk and completely ruined her shoes. She sorted the mail, setting aside the obvious bills. Cullen was sitting in the living room, engrossed in a rerun of *I Love Lucy*, which he'd somehow missed seeing more than twice. He didn't even glance up when she walked through, and Sara was able to slip into her room without being forced to make coherent conversation.

The bills and junk mail were dropped on her dresser with total disregard for her careful sorting. Sitting down on the edge of the bed, she stared at the plain white envelope with that all-important postmark. It had to be from Cody. She'd never seen his handwriting, but that bold scrawl couldn't be anyone else's.

Why had he written? Maybe he had discovered that he loved her after all and he wanted her to come back.

She tried to rein in her excitement. It was probably something more prosaic, like an inquiry about Cullen's health. But wouldn't he have written directly to Cullen for that? Her pulse was pounding so quickly that she felt breathless and the palms of her hands were damp. What if he had written to ask her to come back? She'd go in a minute.

She forced her shaking hands to steady enough to open the envelope. She slid her finger beneath the flap and slowly peeled it upward, drawing out the moment. With the envelope open, she stopped for a moment, drawing a steadying breath before she tilted the envelope and reached inside.

She frowned when she didn't find anything. He couldn't have sent her an empty envelope. Tipping the envelope upside down, she shook it slightly and was rewarded by a shower of paper. She stared down at the scraps, feeling all the excited anticipation turn to a hard lump in her chest. She didn't have to put the torn squares back together to know what she was looking at.

The check she'd mailed to Cody. The check that would have given her at least a fragile connection with his dream. The pain was too much for tears. It was as if he were rejecting her all over again. Her hands shook as she gathered the scraps together and stuffed them back into the envelope. The envelope was stuffed in the back of a drawer. Why she didn't just throw it away was a question she couldn't have answered.

DAVID CAREFULLY ADJUSTED one of the lights, standing back to stare critically at his creation. "Tilt your hand a little, Sara. We want to be sure the diamonds catch the light properly. That's right. Hold that position."

Sara stared out over David's head as he snapped pictures. Her hands were cramping from the awkward position she was holding, but she didn't move. It was all part of the job. The lights that surrounded them were bright enough to make everything beyond a blur, but she didn't care. In the two days since she'd received the check, she found it difficult to care about much of anything.

She lowered her eyes to look down at her hands, carefully posed against a black velvet background. Her nails were perfectly groomed and polished a vivid scarlet red. On the third finger of her left hand, a diamond wedding band caught the light and sent it back in crisp flares of brilliance. The matching diamond engagement ring featured an exquisite stone that seemed to gleam with a life of its own.

Wedding rings. This was the third set she'd modeled this morning. The sparkle of the diamonds seemed to promise hope. Hope for another person. Faith enough to commit yourself to them. Tears blurred her eyes as she stared at the gleaming stones. What would it feel like to walk down the aisle toward the man you loved? To see his face as he turned to look at you?

Tears began to slip down her cheeks. How long was it going to take before she stopped picturing Cody as the loving groom and herself as the bride? Eventually, this pain had to go away. It had to leave her free to fall in love again.

The tears continued to fall and she sniffed quietly. Her hands remained rock steady against the background, and the quiet click and whir of the camera covered the sounds of her silent weeping. It wasn't until David looked up to suggest another pose that he realized anything was wrong.

Sara's eyes were closed, her lashes lying in dark crescents on pale cheeks. Tears dripped steadily from beneath her lashes, trickling down her cheeks to slide off her chin.

"Sara!" He set the camera down and came around the table as she opened her eyes. She sniffed and lifted her hands to her mouth, trying to stop the sobs that threatened to escape.

"I'm sorry, David. I don't know what's the matter with me."

He lifted her to her feet and guided her to his sofa, settling her down into the thick leather depths. Their relationship had been strained. It wasn't easy for him to see her and know that she would never be his, but he cared too much to be unmoved by her obvious pain. He sat down beside her and held her hands, patting them awkwardly while she struggled with her tears, finally winning the battle. He handed her a box of tissues and waited until she had mopped her eyes and blown her nose before he spoke.

"Why don't you go back? You've been miserable ever since you returned from Colorado."

Sara shredded a tissue, unable to deny his words. "He doesn't want me."

"Bull. No man in his right mind wouldn't want you."

She smiled shakily but shook her head. "He doesn't. He tore up my check and sent it back. As if he couldn't even bear to use my money."

"I knew he hadn't cashed it. Did it occur to you that maybe it's his pride? If he cares for you, he's not going to want to use your money."

She sniffed, hope flickering in her eyes before she shook her head again. "If he loved me, he'd have asked me to stay."

"Maybe. People do strange things when they're in love. If you love him, you should go back and tell him how you feel. It's pretty stupid to try and second-guess another person."

"You're awfully sweet, David." Her eyes were a misty violet as she looked at him, and David felt the pain of his loss twist in his guts. "I wish—"

"Don't wish anything." He stood up abruptly. He didn't want her sympathy. "Go back to Colorado and talk to What's-his-name." He picked up a camera and busied himself with an unnecessary change of lenses. "Now, go home. We've got enough pictures for this job."

It seemed as if the world had ganged up on her. Sara drove home, trying not to think about David's words, afraid to hope that they might make sense. She'd no sooner walked in the door and tossed her purse on a chair than Cullen started in on her.

He looked up from the textbook he was reading, his blue eyes skimming her streaked mascara and smudged makeup. He looked her over critically and then slammed his book shut as she sank into a chair across from him.

"You've been crying."

"I...ah...got something in my eye." There were times when Sara wondered which one of them was supposed to be the adult in this family. With his face so stern, Cullen showed a disconcerting resemblance to his father, and Evan had always been able to see through any lie she attempted to tell him.

"When are you going to stop pretending?"

"I don't know what you mean."

"Give it up, Sara. You're miserable and you and I both know it. Why don't you go back to Cody and tell him you love him?"

"Maybe because he didn't ask me to stay," she flared.

"He shouldn't have had to ask. A blind man could have seen how much in love the two of you were. Go back there."

She shifted restlessly, wanting to believe him. "I can't. I've got responsibilities here. I can't just leave you alone and go off to chase a dream."

His eyebrows rose. "It's been a long time since I needed a baby-sitter. I've got this house and Dad left enough money in trust for college. If I resist the urge to buy a Ferrari, I won't even have to work while I go to school. I'm going to be too busy studying to have time for mischief. And I'd love to spend my vacations at the ranch. Don't hide behind me, Sara. You've given me so much already and it means a lot to me that you've always been here for me, but don't use me as an excuse now. It won't wash."

Her eyes shifted away from his and she stood up, smoothing her palms down over her slacks. "I'll think about it."

"You do that. But don't think too long. If you time it right, maybe you can manage to get snowed in with him."

Sara's smile was shaky, but she felt a hint of excitement bubble up in her chest.

Chapter Fourteen

Cody pulled his coat up higher around his ears as he walked to the barn. Under his boots the gravel crunched loudly with each step he took. The sound seemed to echo through the quiet valley. Beneath the brim of his hat, his eyes skimmed the solid blanket of white that coated everything as far as the eye could see. It had stopped snowing only this morning, and so far the blanket was unbroken by so much as a footprint.

Looking at the clouds above, it wasn't hard to predict more snow by nightfall. A lot of it. Another day or two of this and he'd be snowed in for the New Year. It was something that happened at least once each winter, and he was prepared for it. Plenty of food and fuel were stored in the house and barn. He could take just about the worst winter could dish out.

It would be harder for the cattle ranchers. They lost a lot of cattle in a hard winter, but his little herd of horses were easily watched over. With only a few animals, he could keep them closer to home. Even if he was snowed in for weeks, he and the animals would manage all right.

Most winters he didn't mind the isolation. If he'd wanted lots of company, he wouldn't have chosen the business he had. But this winter, loneliness had him by the throat. He stopped and stared up the narrow road that led out of the valley. This winter he already felt cut off from the world.

Sometimes in his days as a financial advisor, he'd felt almost crushing loneliness in the midst of a city bursting with millions. But he'd never felt lonely with just his own company.

He shook his head and started back toward the barn. He was getting maudlin in his old age. Since Sara left... He broke the thought, cursing under his breath. He was beginning to measure everything in terms of before and after Sara. His whole life seemed to have meaning only relevant to when she'd entered it.

Tugging open the barn door, he stepped into the relative warmth, inhaling deeply of the rich scents of hay and horses. Dancer stuck his head over the stall door and nodded a greeting, and Dog wandered over from his bed in one corner and sniffed Cody's hand in greeting.

Looking around at the horses, the neat rows of tack, the fresh hay in the loft, Cody felt a surge of pride. He'd done a lot with this place. A hell of a lot. It had always been enough before. Why did it seem so empty now? Sara's eyes seemed to haunt him. She was in his dreams every night, and even when he was awake, he couldn't stop thinking about her.

He reached down to scratch behind Dog's ear, drawing a sigh of pleasure from the huge animal. "We did okay without her before. We can manage again. I couldn't ask her to stay. I couldn't ask her to give up everything. We were worlds apart. It would never have worked out. Never."

The future stretched out endlessly before him. Cold and empty.

SARA CURSED VIOLENTLY as the car skidded on the road, the rear end sliding toward the ditch. She resisted the urge to brake and steered with the skid, pulling the car straight at the last minute. Outside the windshield, the snow fell in what appeared to be one continuous blanket. Visibility wasn't measured in feet, it was measured in inches.

It seemed days ago that she had rented the four-wheel-drive vehicle in Denver and started out on nice snowplowed roads. It had been snowing when she left, but it hadn't been too bad. The farther north she drove, the worse the storm became. She'd given up listening to the radio. The weather reports were too depressing. If she'd had any sense at all, she would have stopped at the first motel she could find and spent the night there. She could have continued her drive in the morning. But she didn't have any sense, obviously, because here she was driving along with her headlights reflecting off the solid wall of snow in front of her, looking for the road to the Arrow Bar W.

What if she got to the ranch and he wasn't there? What if he was there, but he didn't love her after all? What if they were snowed in together when he didn't love her? She bit her lip to stem the tide of hysterical laughter that bubbled in her throat.

She was exhausted. It had taken two days of begging, pleading and, on occasion, almost threatening for her to get a seat on a flight in the midst of the holiday rush. She hadn't slept since making her decision. She'd used the nighttime hours to pack and repack her suitcases while running over every possible scenario in her mind. It was only years of training that had prevented her from chewing her fingernails to the quick.

Now here she was, in the wilds of northern Colorado, in the middle of a raging blizzard, going to see a man who might or might not love her. She giggled. Since Evan's death she'd walked on a very safe and narrow path. She'd had Cullen to consider. But, when she decided to jump off that safe path, she sure did it with a vengeance.

Now if only she could find the road. When she found it, it was more by instinct than sight. Luckily, there was almost no traffic on the highway, so there was no one to object to her creeping speed as she peered through the darkness, searching for the turnoff.

She turned the wheel slowly, easing off the solid pavement and onto the dirt road, praying that the tires would hold to it. If she'd thought the highway was slick, the word gathered new meaning when she found herself on a road that hadn't seen a snowplow at all.

She lowered her speed until the car was hardly moving, and crept up the hill. Dimly, against the swirling snow, she could make out the outline of the gate. The tires bumped over the cattle guard. She was almost there.

"Come on, baby. Just a little farther." She whispered the words coaxingly. "Just a little ways now."

But it was not to be. It felt as if all four wheels decided to go in separate directions, like a newborn foal trying to find its feet. One minute she was in control, and the next the vehicle was sliding slowly toward the edge of the ditch. There was a bone-jarring jolt as the side wheels slid off the road, and then the car tilted almost gracefully over to rest in the ditch.

Sara sat clutching the now-useless steering wheel, staring out the windshield, trying to decide whether or not anything important was broken. Her fingers were shaking as she reached to turn off the ignition, pocketing the keys absently, though it was unlikely that anyone would be stealing the car in the near future.

It didn't take long to ascertain that she was in one piece, basically uninjured. The same could not be said for the car. What condition it might be in when it was pulled out of the ditch she couldn't even guess, but it certainly wasn't going to be doing her any good now.

She had to scramble across the seat and brace her shoulder against the passenger door to force an exit from the stricken vehicle. She plunged directly into snow past her knees, and the words she muttered threatened to turn the air blue with more than cold. Squinting to see through the storm, she could just make out the lights of the ranch house. They looked warm and cozy and frighteningly far away.

The wind gusted into her, blowing snow down the collar of her coat. She shivered before turning and leaning into the backseat. Her bags had all slid to the other side, and it was several frustrating minutes before she struggled triumphantly up onto the road, her overnight case clutched in one hand and a heavier coat wrapped around her body.

If she'd thought her progress was slow in the car, it was nothing compared to the slowness of her pace on foot. The wind had picked up and seemed to delight in doing its best to knock her over. Snow swirled in front of her eyes, blinding her. She slipped and fell more than once, and each time it was more of an effort to drag herself back to her feet.

She had lots of time to remember every story she'd ever heard about people freezing to death. She kept her eyes peeled wide open, terrified that she would somehow fall asleep on her feet. The third time she fell, she skidded almost a yard on her bottom before she could get her boot heels into the ground to act as a brake. She sat there in the snow, trying to decide whether she should laugh or cry. She was going to feel awfully silly if Cody found her frozen body in the spring thaw, like some kind of macabre Popsicle.

She struggled to her feet again, peering through frozen lashes to make sure that the ranch house was still in front of her. It seemed a little closer now, though that could have been wishful thinking.

Her legs were weak, her boots had long since filled with snow and she was furious with herself. She hadn't planned on landing on his doorstep looking like an orphan of the storm. None of this was going as planned. Tears of exhaustion seeped down her frozen cheeks as she slid her feet carefully along the ground, trying to find patches of ice before they found her.

She managed to go quite a distance before she fell the fourth time. There was no warning. One minute she was standing upright and the next she was having a face-to-face confrontation with a snowdrift. For just a minute, she didn't have the energy to pick herself up. Sheer frustration made her want to scream, and her breath caught on sobs. Nothing was going as she wanted it to.

She closed her eyes. All she wanted was to feel Cody's arms around her and know that she wasn't alone anymore. She opened her eyes and set her jaw, sliding her gloved hands under her body, determined to make it the rest of the way. She hadn't come all this way to tell him she loved him only to freeze to death in front of his house.

Before she could move, strong hands closed around her shoulders, drawing her upright. She didn't even need the shadowy glimpse of his face to know whose hands they were. She gave a sob of relief and flung her arms around Cody's neck as he turned toward the ranch house. Her overnight case was abandoned without another thought.

His steps were slow but confident, and she gave herself up to the safety he offered, knowing that he would take care of her. As if determined to thwart them, the wind picked up, howling down out of the mountains as if a demon were on its heels. Sara buried her face against his shoulder, trying to make herself as light as possible. Beneath her cheek, she could feel his heartbeat, strong and steady.

A trip that would have taken only seconds without the wind and snow dragged out endlessly. Cody tightened his arms around Sara's slight weight as his foot slipped on a patch of ice. She rested in his arms with such total confidence. Even through the howling storm, he almost imagined that he could smell the fresh scent of her hair. Why was she here?

He reached the house at last and mounted the steps, his arms snug around his precious burden. His boot kicked the door open and he stepped into the living room. The silence was profound. Sara hadn't realized how much sheer noise the storm was making until they were shut away from it by the sturdy walls of the house.

Cody kicked the door shut behind them and carried her across the wooden floor, setting her down in front of the fireplace. The heat of the fire was almost painful on her icy cheeks, but it was a good kind of pain.

She glanced up as Cody's fingers began working the buttons of her coat. For a moment, Sara considered telling him that she could manage herself, but it felt good to sit in front of the fire and let him take care of her. Besides, her fingers were so numb she wasn't sure she could manage herself.

He slipped the coat off her shoulders and then disappeared for a few minutes. Sara watched him leave, the anxious feeling in her heart reflected in her eyes. He hadn't said anything. Was he angry with her? Disgusted? She closed her eyes and then opened them to stare into the fire. It was too late to turn back now. She'd made this decision and she just had to believe it was the right one.

When Cody returned, he was carrying a cup of steaming coffee, and a thick terry robe was draped over his arm. He set the coffee down on a scarred end table next to Sara and dropped the robe on a chair.

Sara looked at him as he bent to tug her boots off, but his eyes didn't meet hers. He might have been totally unaware of her, but she didn't believe that. She couldn't believe that. The firelight caught on the chiseled planes of his features, highlighting the stubborn thrust of his jaw. Did he look older than he had? Were the lines beside his mouth a little deeper?

Her boots were set aside and Sara couldn't help her startled gasp when he reached for the bottom of her sweater. Any protest she might have made was lost as he tugged the heavy wool over her head. He stripped her as if she were a child, but Sara said nothing. She caught a glimpse of his face as he reached for the buttons on her shirt and there was nothing in his expression to indicate that he thought of her as childlike.

There was something amazingly erotic about having him undress her in front of the fire while he retained every stitch of clothing. He unsnapped her jeans and slid his hands inside to ease them down over her hips and, as if compelled, his eyes met hers. The fire that burned on the hearth was nothing compared to the green blaze in his eyes, and Sara was suddenly much more confident. He still wanted her. That was something. And he didn't look in the least bit disgusted.

He swallowed hard when she at last stood before him clad only in a tiny pair of violet panties and a matching bra. Sara could see perspiration on his forehead and there was a ragged edge to his breathing. He stared at her slim body for a long moment and then reached for the thick towel he'd brought. His movements were brisk as he rubbed the circulation back into her chilled skin. It wasn't necessary. One look from him and Sara was as warm as if it were a hot summer day, but she said nothing. She liked the feel of his hands on her, even through the heavy towel.

He wrapped her in the terry robe as if putting temptation out of sight, and Sara almost smiled. Her body tingled, both from the rubdown and from his nearness. Neither of them had said a word, but she had to believe that it was going to be all right, that she'd made the right decision.

Cody sat down on a chair opposite the sofa and picked up his own coffee. Sara snuggled back into the worn leather of the sofa and sipped the hot black liquid, staring into the fire. Outside the wind still howled maliciously, but it was cozy and warm inside. For the moment, she was content just to be here with him. This is what it would be like if they were married. Just the two of them sitting next to the fire on a cold winter night.

"Why did you come back?"

The husky question snapped her out of her dream, and tension abruptly lodged in her stomach again. She set the coffee cup down and wrapped her fingers in the belt of the robe, twisting the fabric as she stared at the floor. The moment had arrived. Now was the time to tell him how she felt.

"Sara?" His voice seemed to wrap around her name and she shivered, her eyes meeting his for an instant. It was impossible to read his expression.

"I've done a lot of thinking since I left here." She spoke rapidly, needing to get the words out before she lost her nerve. "I thought about what you said about never asking a woman to give up everything for you. And I thought it might be different if she were to offer."

"Sara..."

She hurried on, wanting to get it all out before he told her it would never work. "I never have really liked modeling. I've worked hard at it, but it wasn't my first love. Cullen has informed me that he no longer needs me to baby-sit him, and I thought maybe it was time to pick up my sculpting again. Denver isn't that far away and there's galleries and classes and stuff there. I could work here and just make the trip to Denver when I had to."

"Sara..."

"This isn't a snap decision. I've thought about it a lot. I think it would work. I don't know much about ranching, but I'd be willing to learn."

"Sara..."

"The thing is, I was miserable in Los Angeles. I missed the quiet and I missed the horses and Dog and . . . I missed you."

"Sara . . ."

She gulped, struggling against the tears that threatened to overflow her eyes. "I love you, Cody." The words came out stark and unadorned, and she bit her lower lip, trying to steady her voice. "I think . . ."

But he didn't seem to want to hear what she thought. He caught her hands and tugged her to her feet, his palm cupping the back of her head, muffling her words in the warm flannel of his shirt. Sara's hands clutched his shoulders. What was he thinking? His hold was strong and tender but he hadn't said anything. Was he trying to find the words to tell her that he loved her or that he didn't? Did he feel sorry for her? She could bear anything but that. If he pitied her, she would run out of the house and take her chances with the storm.

"Didn't you wonder how I knew that you were out in the storm? How I knew you needed me?"

Sara swallowed a sob and shook her head, not lifting her face from his shirt. His fingers slid into her hair, tilting her head back until she looked into his face. The tears in her eyes made it impossible to read his expression. She blinked, trying to clear her vision. There was something there that she'd never seen before.

"I couldn't sleep. All my dreams have been filled with you, but I couldn't read them anymore. But tonight felt different and I didn't dare let myself sleep. I was afraid of what I might dream.

"And then I heard you call my name."

"But I didn't . . ." She stopped, remembering how badly she'd wanted him.

"Didn't you?" His thumb rubbed the delicate line of her jaw, his eyes a deep unfathomable green. "You are the other half of my soul. You are everything I need to make me complete. How could I not know when you needed me?"

"Cody?" Her hand shook as she lifted it to his face, needing to touch him to believe that this was real.

"I love you. I love you so much, it's a constant ache in my gut when you're gone. I hope you know what you're doing because I can't bear to let you go now."

"I don't want you to let me go." She laughed shakily. "I don't want you to ever let me go."

His arms slid around her back, drawing her onto her toes as his head bent to hers. "I won't. I need you too much."

She met his kiss, feeling happiness bloom in her chest and spread in a warm tide throughout her body. They'd gone through a lot to find each other. But he was hers, finally and forever hers. Their kiss deepened, and her hands twined in the thickness of his hair as he sank to his knees, carrying her with him.

The first time they'd come together it had been in a storm, and now another storm raged outside. It seemed fitting that they should make this commitment with the wind howling around the eaves.

She struggled with the buttons on his shirt, feeling the fire hot against her back as he eased the robe open. Storms and fire. She'd come to associate both of them with this man. Never again would she be frightened of either. He'd come into the storm tonight to find her. Stormwalker. Her Stormwalker. Always and forever.